CONTENTS

BIBLE STORY ADVENTURES

FOR KIDS:

The Bible is full of stories from long ago. And while it's fun to learn about the people and the places, it's also important to see how what the Bible says affects the way we live today—especially if we are trying to be friends of Jesus.

Shoebox Kids Bible Stories helps you do both. Every chapter is a double story—first, a story from the Bible, then a story from today that shows one of the lessons that Bible story can teach us. That story—with the Shoebox Kids—is about learning what the Bible really means—at home, at school, or on the playground.

Every story is an adventure in learning to be more like Jesus!

FOR PARENTS AND TEACHERS:

Shoebox Kids Bible Stories does more than just give children information about the Bible—it shows them how to apply that information to everyday life. Teaching our children means going beyond information and entertainment to helping them learn to apply Bible truths. Too many of us grew up learning about the Bible, but not getting to know God. We can help the children we love by showing them not just what the Bible says but what difference it makes in the way we live and love others.

Every Bible story has many lessons to teach, and the Shoebox Kids story can teach only one of those. There may be others you can help your child learn.

The "Questions" at the end of each story can help you see what your child or children understand and what they may be confused about. Many of the questions can be discussion-starters that will help you understand better the children you love. They can help open the doors of communication, which are so important to reassuring them of your love and teaching them about God's.

Jerry D. Thomas

MEET THE SHOEBOX KIDS!

The Shoebox Kids are six friends who go to the same church. Their Sabbath School class meets in a really small room in the church. It's so small, everyone called it "the Shoebox." And their teacher's name is Mrs. Shue (you pronounce it just like "shoe"). So everyone calls them the Shoebox Kids.

Maria and Chris Vargas are Shoebox Kids. They live with their mom and dad and their little sister, Yolanda (everyone calls her Yoyo). Maria is in the fourth grade; Chris is in the third grade. They both are in the same classroom at their small church school.

Jenny Wallace is a Shoebox Kid. Her parents are divorced, and she lives with her mother and her cat, Butterscotch. Her father lives nearby, and she spends many weekends with him. She's in the fourth grade at the local public school.

Sammy Tan is a Shoebox Kid. He lives with his grandparents and is in the fourth grade in the church school. His parents were killed in a car crash when he was very young. He has one uncle.

Willie Teller is a Shoebox Kid. He lives with his parents and his dog, Coco. Willie is handicapped and wheels around in a cool wheelchair. He's in the fourth grade at the same public school as Jenny, but they're not in the same classroom.

DeeDee Adams is a Shoebox Kid. She lives with her parents and her older sister. She's in the third grade at the church school with Chris, Maria, and Sammy.

The Shoebox Kids live in Mill Valley, but they visit a lot of other interesting places. As they study their Bible lesson each week, they find that God is helping them learn about being His friend and treating others like Jesus did.

CHAPTER 1

THE WITCH OF ENDOR
Jesus' Mirror

Samuel was dead. As the people of Israel cried for him and buried him, King Saul was the saddest of all. Without Samuel, how would the king know what God wanted him to do? Saul often didn't listen to Samuel or obey God, but as he chose not to follow God, he got more confused and more scared.

Saul hadn't been a good king. He kept his soldiers so busy chasing David that he wasn't ready when his real enemies came. The Philistines were back, and their army was ready to fight. Saul marched his soldiers into place for a battle, but he didn't know what to do. He prayed, but since he had stopped following God, God did not answer.

One thing Saul had done right—he had chased all the witches, psychics, and fortune-tellers out of Israel, just as God had commanded. Those people said that they could talk to people who had died. Really they couldn't, but Satan used them to confuse people and lead them away from God. So God didn't want those servants of Satan near His people.

But now Saul had given up on God. "Find me a witch or psychic," he told his servants. "I will tell her to ask Samuel what I should do."

His servants searched until they found a witch near Endor. Then Saul put on plain clothes and went quietly to the witch. "I need to talk to someone who is dead," Saul said to her. "Can you help me?"

"I can't do that," the woman answered. "The king won't allow anyone who does that to live in Israel. I would be arrested and killed."

"I promise that nothing will happen to you," Saul said. "Bring up Samuel the prophet."

Now the woman recognized Saul. "You're the king! You'll have your soldiers kill me if I do this."

"No," Saul said, "I won't. Now tell me what you see."

The woman closed her eyes for a moment. "I see someone coming up from the ground," she said. "It is an old man wearing a cloak."

Saul was sure that she saw Samuel. He fell down and covered his face.

Then a voice spoke to Saul. It wasn't Samuel, but one of Satan's angels pretending to be Samuel. "Why are you disturbing me?" the voice asked.

"I need help," Saul answered. "The Philistines are attacking, and God won't answer my prayers. Tell me what to do."

"Why are you asking me?" the voice said. "God is doing just what He said He would do. He is giving the kingdom to David. Since you wouldn't obey Him, He is giving Israel to the Philistines. Tomorrow, you and your sons will be joining me in the grave."

When he heard this terrible news, Saul fell over on the ground. The witch was afraid that he would die right there. She fixed food for him and his servants so they would have enough strength to leave.

When the battle began the next day, Saul had no hope of winning. His soldiers ran away scared. Jonathan and two of his other sons fought bravely, but they were killed. Saul was wounded badly by arrows. "Take my sword and kill me before the Philistines can capture me," he told his bodyguard. But the bodyguard was too scared to do it. So Saul stood his sword up, then fell on it, and died.

Saul could have been a great king, but he wouldn't listen to God or obey Him. Finally, when God wouldn't talk to him anymore, Saul turned to Satan's servants for help. How sad an ending for someone who was chosen by God to be Israel's first king!

Jesus' Mirror

Swish-plink! Harvey the wizard swished his wand through the air as he spoke the magic words. "Rollypollus!" Two bad guys and their dangerous weapons went tumbling backwards.

"Chris."

Chris Vargas didn't even hear his mother's voice. As usual, after a hard day in third grade, he was home watching some after-school cartoons. On the screen, Harvey dropped a large bucket of paint over the head of one bad guy and sent a big paintbrush to chase their leader, Brillo. Chris laughed when the paintbrush tripped up Brillo and painted him orange.

"Chris?"

This time Chris heard his mother and frowned. *I'll pretend I don't hear her until the next commercial,* he said to himself. On TV, Harvey jumped straight up just in time as two guys who were chasing him crashed into each other. But then his wand flew out of his hand! Brillo had his book of spells out, and he was doing magic too! Quickly, Harvey spoke the word to make people disappear.

"Disappearo!"

Snap! The TV clicked off.

"Chris!" Mrs. Vargas stood between Chris and the TV, holding a stack of papers and books. "This is the third time I've called you. What kind of cartoon are you watching that makes you ignore your mother?"

"Aw, Mom. It was just Harvey Peter," Chris said.

"Is that the show with all that fighting? Chris, I don't think I like you watching that."

"They're helping others, Mom. Today, Brillo was trying to paint the White House red! The president called Harvey to stop him." Chris didn't mention the magic and spells that were in the show. He knew his mother wouldn't like that.

Mrs. Vargas frowned. "Chris, I think you and your sisters watch too many of these cartoons. Are you being careful to put only things in your mind that will make you more like Jesus?" She dropped part of her stack in Chris's lap. "Here's your Sabbath School lesson book. Would you please put it in your room?"

Jesus' Mirror

Chris thought about what his mother had said. He really did want to be like Jesus. Could watching a few cartoons make any difference? He grabbed up his Primary lesson book and flipped it open to that week's story. It was about Satan's tricks. After reading for a minute, he shook his head. "Mom, I know this cartoon stuff is all fake. I know it's just a show."

"Well, that's enough cartoons for today anyway," she said. "Why don't you go and clean your room? Your cousins should be here in a few minutes. They're going to want to play with you."

You mean they're going to want to bother me, Chris said to himself. *I wish I could just watch cartoons today. I bet no one ever bothers Harvey like this.*

He frowned and headed to his room.

That next Sabbath, the first thing Chris noticed when he walked into the Shoebox was an orange blanket hanging on the front wall like it was covering something. "Good morning, Mrs. Shue," Chris called to his teacher. He started to ask about the blanket, but his sister Maria burst through the door with Jenny. The two girls ran over next to DeeDee. Chris stepped out of their way and then sat beside Sammy and Willie.

Mrs. Shue was ready to begin. "This quarter we're going to do something different. One of the things I like most about teaching this class is watching you grow into happy Christians, to see each of you becoming more like Jesus every week."

Chris looked at Mrs. Shue with a big question mark on his face. So did everyone else.

Mrs. Shue laughed. "No, I haven't lost my marbles. Each of you really is changing. And this quarter, I want to help you notice it happening." She walked over to the orange blanket and carefully pulled it loose so that it dropped to the floor.

There on the wall was a fancy, old-fashioned mirror. It had a large wooden frame, and at the top was a picture of Jesus and a sign that read, "Jesus' Mirror."

"Every week, we'll be learning from the stories in the Bible. If you see that you've learned an important lesson, tell me, and we'll put your name up here beside the mirror. At the end of the quarter, you'll be able to look up here and see how much you have grown."

Chris raised his hand. "Mrs. Shue, I learned something from our lesson this week."

"Tell us about it, Chris."

"Well, you know our lesson was about Satan's tricks and how he fooled King Saul into asking a witch to bring up the ghost of Samuel to talk to. I figured that it didn't have much to do with me. But I was wrong."

Then Chris told them about his cousins and how much they had bothered him while he was playing. "They were such a pain, I just wanted them to disappear. So, without even thinking, I said 'Disappearo!' "

Willie and Jenny nodded. They recognized the word. The others looked confused. "It's from Harvey the wizard," Willie told them. "It's the magic word he uses to make the bad guys disappear."

"That's right," Chris said. "I didn't think there was anything wrong with that cartoon, but Satan was trying to

use it to fool me into asking him for special magic pow-
ers."

"Wow!" Sammy said. "I never thought of it that way,
but you're right. Satan is tricking us into using his words
and his ways of treating people."

"You really did learn an important lesson, Chris," Mrs.
Shue said. "Come up here to the mirror. Chris, I believe
that this week you are looking less like King Saul. He fell
for Satan's tricks, and you didn't. You are becoming more
like David, who was learning to listen to God."

Chris looked in the mirror and smiled. Maybe Mrs. Shue
was right. Maybe he was changing. He could hardly wait
to watch and see.

QUESTIONS

1. What are some of your favorite cartoon or other TV
shows? Why do you like them?

2. Are the things you watch and do making you more
like Jesus?

3. Can you think of any other ways besides cartoons
that Satan is trying to trick us?

4. Are you changing every week? Are you sure? Ask a
parent or teacher what they think!

5. Do you want to be more like Jesus?

DAVID BECOMES KING; UZZAH DIES
Someone In Charge

David was hiding from Saul in the city of Ziklag when the Philistines attacked Israel, so he wasn't in the battle. When David heard that King Saul and his friend Jonathan were dead, he cried and tore his clothes. After the time for mourning was past, David asked God, "Should I go back home to Judah?" David's family was from the tribe of Judah.

"Yes," God answered. "Go to the city of Hebron."

When David arrived in Hebron, the men of the tribe of Judah crowned him king. But the rest of the tribes of Israel made Ish-Bosheth, one of Saul's sons, king. For seven years there was fighting between the men from Judah and the men from the other tribes. But many people remembered that Samuel had anointed David king, and when Ish-Bosheth was killed, all the tribes joined together to make David king.

David wanted a new, strong city to be his home. He wanted the city of Jerusalem. But the Jebusites lived in that city and it was protected by strong walls that no army could get past. David didn't give up—he came up with a clever plan to get past the walls. He led his soldiers through the water tunnels under the city and came up inside. After a short battle, the city was his!

As soon as his new palace was built—with help from Hiram, king of Tyre—David wanted to bring God's ark to Jerusalem. Many years before, it had been taken by the Philistines. When they sent it back, the ark ended up at the house of Abinadab. It was still there.

So David made a special holiday for the moving of the ark. Thousands of people went with him to Abinadab's house. They put the ark on a special new cart that was pulled by oxen. Uzzah and Ahio, two of Abinadab's sons, led the way as they headed back toward Jerusalem.

As the cart crossed over a wheat-threshing floor, it hit a bump and tilted. The ark started to slide off the cart! When he saw what was happening, Uzzah reached up and grabbed the ark to keep it steady. But as soon as he touched the ark, he was struck dead!

David stopped the cart. All the people were afraid and confused. David was very upset. "Why has God done this?" he asked.

Both Uzzah and David should have known that no one was supposed to touch God's holy ark. Only the priests could move it from one place to another.

David was afraid to take the ark on to Jerusalem now. He left it at the home of Obed-edom, who lived nearby. The ark stayed there for three months while David tried to decide whether God wanted the ark in Jerusalem. But someone said, "Look how much Obed-edom's family has been blessed! God must want to bless Jerusalem that way."

So David went back to get the ark. This time, priests carried it just the way Moses and Aaron had been taught back when the ark was first made. They stopped to pray and worship, taking only a few steps at a time. This time, David wanted to show his respect for God by moving the ark exactly as God had instructed.

Someone In Charge

"**I** don't care! I don't have to, and you can't make me!"

DeeDee's mouth fell open. She had never heard any-one talk to their mother like that. She turned her back to Morgan and her mother and stared at a shelf full of books, pretending to be reading the titles.

"Morgan," Mrs. Harcomb repeated, "I just want you to put away your dolls before you get out your kitchen toys." Morgan didn't say anything. She just kept stacking up her plastic pans and dishes. DeeDee heard Mrs. Harcomb sigh and leave the room.

As soon as the door closed, Morgan hopped over to where DeeDee stood. "Do you want to go jump on the trampoline?" she asked with a big grin.

DeeDee was surprised. "Shouldn't we put these toys away first? Your mother will be upset if we don't."

Morgan laughed. "She's always upset about some-thing."

"But won't you get in trouble?" DeeDee started picking up the dolls as she talked.

"No. I do whatever I want. Let's sneak out the back way."

DeeDee wasn't sure what to do, but she dropped the dolls and followed Morgan. Later, they ran into the kitchen, and Morgan shouted at her mother, "We're thirsty! What is there to drink?"

Mrs. Harcomb and DeeDee's mother were nearby in the living room talking. "Have some nice grape juice or some milk, dear. It's all there in the refrigerator."

DeeDee followed Morgan to the refrigerator. "Look, there's a can of root beer," Morgan said. "Let's share that."

"But . . ." DeeDee started to remind Morgan that her mother had said juice or milk, but she remembered that it didn't matter to Morgan. "OK."

Just then, DeeDee heard the front door slam and Mrs. Harcomb's voice call out, "There you are, Charles. I've been worried about you. Say Hello to my friend, Mrs. Adams."

DeeDee heard a grunt, and then Charles, Morgan's fifteen-year-old brother, was in the kitchen. He went straight to the refrigerator, brushing Morgan away from the door. Then he saw the can of root beer in her hand. "Just what I wanted," he said as he snatched it away.

"Hey, give that back! We were going to drink that."

Charles ignored Morgan's shouting and walked away.

"Mom, make him give it back! I wanted that root beer. He took it from me." Morgan followed him into the living room, still shouting.

"Charles," Mrs. Harcomb called out, "if she had it first, then please give it back to her." Charles just kept walking without saying anything. He disappeared down the hall.

"Mom!"

DeeDee went over to stand by her mother, who was pretending to read a magazine. Mrs. Harcomb sighed and put her hand to her head. "Please find something else, Morgan. We have enough to drink in this house. We don't need to fight about it."

"Oh, Mother," Morgan snapped, "you let him get away with anything." She stamped her feet back to the kitchen.

Mrs. Harcomb looked up at DeeDee's mother. "Sorry about that," she said. "Teenagers can be so much trouble."

"I understand," Mrs. Adams said. "We do need to be going anyway. DeeDee, are you ready?"

"Yes, Mother," DeeDee hoped she didn't sound too happy, but she was glad to leave.

Later, in the car, DeeDee asked, "What was wrong with them?"

"Didn't they seem happy to you?"

"No. Morgan was screaming at her mother. Her mother looked like she had a headache most of the time, and Charles was mean to Morgan and their mother."

Mrs. Adams glanced over at DeeDee. "What do you mean?"

DeeDee frowned. "He took Morgan's drink. That was mean and selfish. And then he ignored Mrs. Harcomb when she asked him to give it back."

"Was Morgan any better?"

"No," DeeDee remembered. "She ignored her mother,

too, and did whatever she wanted. She said her mother never did anything about it when she disobeyed."

Her mother looked sad. "Do you wish you lived in a home where you could do whatever you wanted?"

"I used to think so, but not if that's what it would be like. And if they acted like that with guests around, it must really be bad when they are alone." DeeDee thought about Morgan and her brother. "But Mother, why do they treat their mother that way? Don't they love her?"

"I'm sure they do, DeeDee," her mother answered as she signaled to turn left. "But they don't respect her. They've learned that they can do whatever they want, and even if they disobey her, nothing happens. The big problem in that house, DeeDee, is that no one is in charge."

"Respect means listening to the person in charge?"

"That's right. Even when you don't understand why."

DeeDee thought about that. "And respecting God is the same thing. We listen to Him, because He's in charge of the whole world."

"You're right again, DeeDee," her mother said.

DeeDee laughed. "And I thought that living in a house with no rules, where no one was in charge, would be fun! Boy, was I wrong! I sure am glad that there is Someone in charge of the whole world."

She told the story to her Shoebox friends that Sabbath. "I guess it helps me understand the story of Uzzah. Uzzah wasn't just trying to keep the ark from falling over. He was breaking a rule God had given. If nothing had happened, then Uzzah and King David and all the people would have lost respect for God."

Sammy agreed. "They might have thought that there really wasn't a real God. They would have thought that no one was in charge."

"I see we have all learned something this week," Mrs. Shue said. "And DeeDee, look," she added, pointing to the big mirror she called Jesus' Mirror. Mrs. Shue wanted the Shoebox Kids to see whether they were looking more like the Bible people they studied each week. She wanted them to see that they were changing and becoming more like Jesus.

"What?" DeeDee asked, trying to see what was in the mirror.

"This week, you don't look like Uzzah at all!"

QUESTIONS

1. Have you ever heard someone talk to their parent like Morgan did? Have you ever talked like that?

2. Why would a family be unhappy if no one was in charge?

3. What does respect mean?

4. How can we show respect for God?

5. Will you help make your home happy this week by showing respect to your parents?

CHAPTER

DAVID'S PROMISE
Keeping a Promise

King David walked through his palace one day, remembering when he was young and had first come to King Saul's palace. He remembered his friend Jonathan. His friend had died fighting the Philistines, but David remembered a promise they had made each other.

"Let's promise that we will always be friends and that we will always take care of each other's families," Jonathan had said. David had promised his friend. Now he thought to himself, *I wonder if anyone from Jonathan's family is still alive?*

He asked people around the palace. "Is there anyone left alive from Jonathan's family?"

No one knew. But someone said, "Ziba might know."

"Who is Ziba?" David asked.

"Ziba and his family were servants of Saul long ago. He might know if Jonathan or anyone from Saul's family is still alive."

David clapped his hands. "Send for Ziba right away!" he commanded.

When Ziba arrived at the palace, David went straight to him. "Is there anyone still alive from Jonathan's family?" he asked Ziba. "I want to keep my promise to him and take care of his family if I can."

Ziba listened, then nodded slowly. "Jonathan's son Mephibosheth is alive."

David could hardly believe his ears. "Mephibosheth? Tell me—where is he? Is he well?"

Ziba told the story. "Mephibosheth was five years old the day that King Saul and Jonathan were killed in battle. Everyone in the palace was scared when the news came. No one knew what would happen to them. Mephibosheth's nurse picked him up as the family ran away. But in her hurry, she stumbled and fell. She dropped little Mephibosheth, and his feet were badly hurt. From that day on, he has been able to walk only with crutches."

David jumped to his feet. "Go and find Mephibosheth and bring him to the palace," he commanded his soldiers. The soldiers marched to the village where Mephibosheth lived and insisted that he come with them to David's palace.

Mephibosheth was worried. All he knew about David was that King Saul had hated him. He was afraid that David might want him dead! He worried about his family and his son, Micha. Would the new king kill them all?

When Mephibosheth got to David's palace, he fell down on his face in front of the king. "No, no," David said. "Don't be afraid of me. Your father was my best friend. I want to keep my promise to him. I am giving you all the land that once belonged to him and to your grandfather, King Saul."

Now Mephibosheth could hardly believe his ears! But David wasn't finished. He said, "And you, Mephibosheth, are always welcome to eat at the table with my family."

This was a great honor. "Thank you," Mephibosheth said. "You are being very kind to me. I will be your servant forever."

"No, no," David said with a smile. Then he called to Ziba. "Ziba, you and your family served Saul. Now I want you to serve Mephibosheth. Farm his land and harvest his crops. Care for him like you did for King Saul."

So Ziba and his big family moved to Mephibosheth's new farm and took care of it for him. Mephibosheth stayed at the palace and was treated like family from that day on.

David kept his promise to his friend.

Keeping a Promise

"**N**o, not by him. Let's sit over there."

It was a whisper, but it was a loud one that everyone on that end of the playground could hear. Sammy turned his face away. He knew whom they were talking about. It was always the same. It was Marshall.

Sammy opened his lunch bag and pulled out his sandwich. He liked it when Mrs. Peterson let them eat lunch outside. It was a little chilly out, but the sun was shining, and it felt good to be outside for a while. While he chewed his sandwich, he looked at Marshall and shook his head.

No one sat by Marshall. No one played with him if they could help it. Usually, if someone spoke to him, it was to make fun of him. Mostly, he hung around the teacher.

Sammy didn't like Marshall either. He wasn't exactly sure why, but he didn't. Maybe it was just because Marshall was a nerd. He was clumsy and sloppy and never knew when to keep his mouth shut. Still, he had never done anything to Sammy.

Sammy never did anything mean to Marshall. Mostly, he just ignored him. Of course, when he was captain of the kickball team, he didn't pick Marshall if he could help it, but no one did. Still, he helped Marshall once in a while with math—that is, when Mrs. Peterson asked him to.

It's been this way all year, Sammy thought as he peeled his orange. *So why does it bother me today?* Then he remembered what Mrs. Shue had said in Sabbath School that week.

"David and Jonathan were friends," she said. "Even though David wasn't the king yet, he promised Jonathan that he would always take care of him and his family. Now after King Saul and Jonathan were dead and David was king, people thought that David would want to get rid of all Saul's family."

"Why would he do that?" Chris had asked.

"So that none of them would try to become king. But David remembered his promise to Jonathan. And when he found out that Jonathan had a son . . . DeeDee, I know you remember this name."

"Me-phib-o-sheth (meh-fib-o-sheth)," DeeDee said carefully.

28

"That's right," Mrs. Shue had agreed. "When David found Mephibosheth, he moved him right into the palace and gave him all the riches of Saul's family. Now, Willie, what did Mephibosheth do to deserve to be treated so nicely?"

Willie had a puzzled look on his face. "Well, nothing, I guess. David was just keeping his promise to Jonathan."

"Right. David didn't wait to see if Meph was a lot of fun to be around or really popular or just a nerd that no one liked. He kept his promise. Now what can we learn from that? Have we made a promise to be kind?"

Sammy had answered that one. "To be Christians, don't we sort of promise to be like Jesus, to be kind to everyone?" Everyone had agreed. Sammy wondered if they were still thinking about it like he was.

Sammy wadded up his paper bag and tossed it into the trashcan. He walked to the door and lined up with the rest of the third and fourth graders. *Mrs. Shue said that sometimes we have to be kind to people because of our promise to Jesus, not because of the way they act,* he remembered. *Does that mean people like Marshall?*

Later, during Math, Mrs. Peterson asked him to help Marshall with his multiplication. When he moved his chair over to Marshall's desk, he saw Jason roll his eyes and laugh. Sammy knew Jason was thinking: *Marshall is so dumb he needs help in math.* Sammy knew that last week, he would have laughed at Marshall, too. But this time he thought about it. *I've seen Jason ask Jenny for help with English,* he remembered. *Why is it different for Marshall?*

He knew the answer. *Only because no one likes Marshall,* he thought. *And didn't I promise to be kind to everyone, like Jesus was?* He turned and smiled at Marshall. "What are we working on?"

Marshall's face lit up like no one had smiled at him in a long time. "I can't get this problem right. I've tried three times."

"Let's start at the beginning," Sammy said. By recess time, Marshall had done most of the page correctly.

"Thanks, Sammy. I think I understand now. You're a good teacher," Marshall said as he put his book away. Sammy looked at Marshall and made up his mind. "Marshall, you want to play catch this recess?"

"Really? Sure, that would be great."

Sammy grabbed his glove and headed out. "Come on, Sammy, be on our team," someone called from the baseball field. He just waved and turned away. He looked up to see a ball flying right at his head. He jerked up his glove just in time.

"Hey," he said, "be careful." He tossed it back to Marshall, who was laughing. After a few catches, Marshall was ready to try another trick.

"I'll show you how hard I can pitch," he shouted. Then he wound up like a windmill and let the ball go. It sailed way over Sammy's head. Sammy just looked at Marshall for a second, then walked back to pick it up.

"One more try," Marshall shouted, starting to wind up.

"No," Sammy shouted, "just throw it." But it was already on its way past him, out toward the ball field.

He threw down his glove and walked after it. *This is going to be harder than I thought,* he said to himself. Before he got to the ball, Jason picked it up and tossed it to him.

"Tough luck having to play with Marshall," he said. "Is Mrs. Peterson making you do it?"

Sammy had to stop and think. "No, she's not. I'm just trying to be nice."

"You're not turning into a nerd, too, are you?" Jason asked. Then he walked back to the game.

This is going to be a lot harder than I thought, Sammy said to himself, staring after Jason. Walking back toward Marshall, he was glad to hear Mrs. Peterson blow the whistle that ended recess. He had a lot to think about.

Is it worth it? he asked himself as he colored a chart during art. *Marshall really is a pain, and Jason and the other guys will think I'm becoming a nerd. But what about my promise to be like Jesus?* Sammy didn't know what to do, but he held the marker still for just a few seconds and prayed.

Later, after school, Jason met him at the door. "So, are you playing ball with us tomorrow afternoon?"

"Yes," Sammy said. "I'll be there."

When Marshall came out of the building, alone as usual, Sammy was waiting. "Hey, Marshall, if Mrs. Peterson lets us eat outside tomorrow, let's play catch after we eat."

"Really? That would be great, Sammy," Marshall looked really happy.

"But no more fast pitches," Sammy warned.

"OK. See you tomorrow."

DAVID'S PROMISE

The next Sabbath, Sammy was in the Shoebox before anyone, even Mrs. Shue. When she came in, he was looking in the big mirror. "Good morning, Sammy. Who are you looking like in Jesus' Mirror this Sabbath?"

Sammy laughed. "I'm trying to see if I look a little bit like David."

"And do you?"

"Maybe," Sammy said. "Maybe just a little."

QUESTIONS

1. How do you feel when you are picked on or left out?

2. Is there someone like Marshall in your school? How many friends does he or she have?

3. What did Sammy do to try to keep his promise to be like Jesus?

4. What does it mean when Christians make a promise to be like Jesus?

5. Will it be easy for Sammy to be nice to Marshall? Will it be easy for you to be nice to the person in your school that no one likes?

6. Will you keep your promise to be like Jesus?

DAVID'S SON ABSALOM
Roller-Skate Rescue

David was a good king, but sometimes he stopped listening to God and did whatever he wanted. He did some bad things. He had several wives already, but one day he saw a beautiful woman and wanted to marry her also. But she was already married to one of his soldiers. David sent that soldier to a very dangerous place in a battle so he would be killed. Then he married the woman.

David thought no one knew what he had done, but God knew. God sent a prophet to tell everyone what the king had done. David listened to the prophet and to God. He was very sorry for his sin. God forgave David, but He knew that there would be problems because of David's bad example.

David didn't teach his children very well. His sons learned that they could do whatever they wanted. They fought with one another. Amnon attacked his sister. Absalom hated Amnon for that and later had him killed. David loved his son Absalom, but he sent him away from the palace for years. But, finally, David forgave Absalom and let him come back to Jerusalem to live.

Now Absalom was handsome and popular. But he was also sneaky. He wanted to be king instead of his father. He rode around the city in a big chariot as if he were already the king. He went down to the city gate every day and listened to the people's complaints. "If I were the king, I could help you," he would say. "Too bad I'm not the king." He was trying to make the people think he should be king. He wanted the people to love him more than they loved David.

And it worked. Many people wished Absalom were king instead of his father. When enough soldiers and fighters were on his side, Absalom was ready. He had all his followers meet him secretly in Hebron. There he had himself crowned king, and he led his army back to Jerusalem to fight David, his father.

When David heard, he ordered all his soldiers and friends out of the city. He didn't want there to be any fighting in Jerusalem. He ordered the priests to keep God's ark in the city, also.

Absalom was surprised to find no one to fight when he arrived. By the time he sent his soldiers after David, David's army was ready. David wanted to win the battle, but he still loved his son. He told his generals, "If you find Absalom, don't hurt him."

Absalom's soldiers weren't ready for the battle. Soon they were all running away. Absalom was riding away on his mule when he ducked under a tree branch. Somehow, his head got caught in the branches. The mule kept running, leaving Absalom hanging in the middle of the air!

Before long, one of David's soldiers saw Absalom. He told Joab, one of the generals. Joab knew what David had said about not hurting Absalom, but he also knew that Absalom was a dangerous man. He killed Absalom with a spear.

The battle was over quickly. A messenger ran to tell David. "Your soldiers have won!" he told the king.

"What about my son?" David asked. "Is Absalom safe?"

The messenger chose the nicest words he could say. "May all your enemies be like Absalom," he said.

David threw back his head and cried for his son.

Absalom could have been a great leader, but he didn't honor God or his parents. He wasted his life and hurt the ones who loved him most.

Roller-Skate Rescue

"**O**h, please, oh please, oh please, oh please!"

Maria loved to roller skate. She would do almost anything to go, including begging her mother—like she was doing now. "We won't be gone long, and Emily's mother will take us. And you know that the Jacksons will be there." Mrs. Jackson was a teacher in the church's youth department and a friend of Maria's family.

Mrs. Vargas listened with a kind of frown on her face. Then she said, "If you'll hush for just a minute so I can think . . ."

Maria zipped her lips. She really did want to go. She had never been to the Roller-Rama to skate. In fact, she had never been skating with Emily at all. Emily lived down the street, and they played together sometimes, but they weren't really good friends.

"Maria, I don't know Emily's mother very well. Are you sure she wants to take you?"

"Mom, I was there when Emily asked her. She'll drop us off for two hours while she is shopping. Can I go?"

"I'm not sure I like you going to the Roller-Rama. But since the Jacksons will be there, and if Emily's mother is taking you, I guess you can go. But Maria . . ." She was talking to Maria's back now. Maria was busy digging in her closet for her skates with the neon green wheels. "Maria!"

"Yes, Mom?" Maria popped out with a skate in each hand.

"I don't want you to go outside of the skating rink. You go straight in to skate and wait inside when it's time for Emily's mom to pick you up."

"Sure, Mom. No problem." Maria didn't know what her mother was worried about, but she would agree to wait standing on her head if she had to.

The rink was crowded with laughing, shouting, screaming kids. Maria especially liked the speed-skating time. When they announced skating for couples, she split to the side for a drink.

"Whoa!" Emily shouted as Maria flew up to her and some of her friends. And Maria turned and stopped, just like she planned. Except her long, dark hair flew right into her face. "You're a great skater," Emily said.

"I roller skate a lot," Maria said with smile. "It's my favorite thing to do." She saw one of Emily's friends roll his eyes up like he thought she was crazy.

"Let's go," said another girl standing nearby. Maria noticed that Emily's friends weren't even wearing skates. "Are you coming, Emily?"

They looked at Emily, and Emily looked at Maria. "Do you want to go across the street and get some ice cream or something?"

Maria looked at Emily's friends. They were older, maybe fifth or sixth graders. Ice cream sounded good, but . . . then she remembered what her mother had said. "No, I'd rather skate. Come on, Emily, I'll race you around." Then she turned and took off.

About halfway around the rink, Emily cut across and skated up to her. "Thanks for helping me out there," she shouted over the noise of the skaters.

"What?" Maria asked. "What did I do?" They swerved to miss a pileup of little kids.

"You gave me a good reason not to go with them." They sped around a couple who was too busy holding hands to skate straight.

"Why didn't you want to go with them?" Maria asked.

"They're older than me, and sometimes they get in trouble. My mom doesn't like them at all. If she knew they hung around here, she wouldn't even let me skate at this rink."

Maria shook her head. "Then why are they your friends?"

"I don't know," Emily said. "They're just cool, I guess."

Near the end of their two hours, Emily and Maria sat down to take off their skates. "Whoa," Maria said when she stood up. "I always have trouble remembering how to walk again."

"Let's go get a drink at the ice-cream shop," Emily suggested as she slipped on her shoes.

"Sure," Maria said, and they headed for the door. Suddenly, she remembered. "Wait, Emily. I think I'll stay here."

"Why?"

"I told my mom that I'd wait for your mother inside the skating rink."

"So? We'll just wait for her over there. It's no big deal," Emily said as she held the door open. "You coming?"

Maria put her hand on the door, but . . . "No, I'll wait here. I told her I would."

Emily shrugged her shoulders and turned to cross the parking lot. Suddenly, a police car flashed around the corner and skidded to a stop. The officers ran toward the ice-cream shop. Two kids inside flew out the door and took off down the street with the police right behind. A second police car pulled up beside the first.

Emily jumped back inside. "Did you see that?" she gasped.

"Wasn't that your friends?"

Emily just nodded and stared down the street. Her mother pulled up, but stopped to talk to the police officer in the second car. When she drove to the front of the skating rink door, Maria and Emily jumped in.

"Do you see that?" Emily's mom asked, pointing to the police car. "Right here in front of the skating rink, kids are selling drugs! You're not skating here ever again, Emily. Sorry about this, Maria."

At home, Maria went straight to her mother and hugged her tight. "Boy, am I glad I listened to you tonight, Mom."

That week in Sabbath School, Mrs. Shue set up the story of King David and Absalom like a play, with a wig of long hair for Chris to wear while he played Absalom. Maria laughed to see Chris's hair caught in a clothes hanger that was supposed to be a tree limb.

"Absalom never learned to respect and obey his father," Mrs. Shue said. Maria raised her hand. "Yes, Maria?"

"I learned something about obeying my parents this week." Then she told them the story of the skating trip.

"I heard about that on the news," Mrs. Shue said. "I'm so glad you obeyed your mother."

"So am I," Maria agreed. She looked up at Mrs. Shue's big mirror at the front of the room and the sign over it that said, "Jesus' Mirror." She saw her reflection and smiled. "At least I know I don't look more like Absalom this week."

"Well," Willie said, holding up Chris's wig, "you do have hair like Absalom." Everyone laughed.

Maria held up her head. "Well, I guess Absalom should have had roller skates like me."

DAVID'S SON ABSALOM

QUESTIONS

1. What was good about the way Maria handled Emily's friends?

2. Why should you obey your parents even when they don't explain?

3. How are you becoming less like Absalom and more like Jesus?

5
CHAPTER

THE WISEST MAN IN THE WORLD
Solomon's Twin Brother

When King David was very old, people began to wonder who would be king after he died. Once David had promised that his son Solomon would be king. But his oldest son, Adonijah, decided that he should be king instead. He decided to gather all the people who supported him and announce that he had been crowned the new king.

But the prophet Nathan heard about the plan. He told David what Adonijah was planning. He reminded David that it was God's plan for Solomon to be the next king. So David crowned Solomon king that very day.

Later, after David died, Solomon went to the town of Gibeon to pray and ask God for help in running the kingdom. God spoke to Solomon. "What shall I give you?" God asked.

Solomon said, "I don't know what to do to be a good king. I feel like a child. Please give me wisdom so I can rule my people fairly and know the difference between good and evil."

Solomon's answer made God very happy. "Because you asked for wisdom instead of money or a long life, I will give you those things also. You will have more money and more honor than any other king."

So Solomon became the wisest man in the world. Everyone brought his or her problems to him to solve. One day, two women came to him. They lived together, and each one had a baby. The first woman told Solomon, "One night, that woman's baby died. While I was asleep, she took my baby and put the dead baby in my bed."

"No," the second woman shouted. "That's a lie. My baby is alive. Her baby died."

"No, my baby is the living one," the first one shouted.

Everyone watched to see what King Solomon would do. "Bring me a sword," he said. A soldier rushed forward with a sharp sword. "Now," King Solomon said, "cut the baby in two and give half to each woman."

"No, no," the first woman cried. "Let her have the baby. Just don't kill it."

The second woman shrugged. "Go ahead and cut it in two. Then no one will have a baby."

King Solomon stood up. "Give the baby to the first woman," he commanded. "She is the real mother." Solomon knew that the real mother would give her baby away to save its life.

Everyone was talking about Solomon's wisdom. Stories about him spread to countries far away. The queen of Sheba heard about Solomon and wanted to meet this wise man. She traveled to Jerusalem and brought gifts for the king.

The queen asked Solomon many hard questions, and he answered every one. "I didn't believe anyone could be so wise," she said. "Your God must be very happy with you."

God *was* very happy with Solomon. Because he asked for wisdom, he became the greatest king Israel ever had.

Solomon's Twin Brother

Willie rolled down the aisle towards the sports department, holding his breath. Then he saw it. One whole row of baseball gloves, and they were all on sale!

"Dad," he called back over his shoulder, "here they are, just like Sammy said. May I buy one?"

Mr. Teller followed Willie down the aisle. "This is the right time of year to buy a glove. These are good prices. With your birthday money, you could buy almost any one of these."

"All right!" Willie said as he pushed himself along the row. He stared at the gloves, then picked out one to try on. "This one's nice, but not quite big enough," he said to his dad. He tried on a couple more, then he saw the glove he wanted. It looked perfect. He grabbed it and tried it on.

"Look, Dad. It's perfect. It's real leather, and it has a deep pocket." Willie smiled and pounded his fist into the glove. "It's an All-Star glove," he added, pointing to the words written along the thumb.

"This is a nice one," his dad agreed. He tried it on, too, and flexed his fingers to open and close it. "It would last a long time if you took care of it. But look," he pointed out, "it costs more than the others."

Willie looked at the price tag. It did cost more than the other gloves. It cost five dollars more than he had. "That is a lot of money," he said out loud.

"Maybe you should look at the other gloves again," his dad said.

Willie looked at the others, but he kept the All-Star glove in his hands. Those other gloves just didn't look as good as the All-Star one. He made up his mind. "No. This is the one I want. Will you pay the other five dollars, Dad?"

Mr. Teller thought for a minute. Then he shook his head. "No. I want you to pay for this glove with your own money. But I will do this. The glove will be on sale for one more week. I'll give you enough extra chores and work this week so that you can earn the money, and then we'll come back and get it."

Willie frowned. He didn't want to put the glove back down. He wanted to take it home now. But he knew his dad's plan was a good idea. "OK, I'll do it." They were on their way out when Willie spotted some baseball cards.

"Wait a minute, Dad. I want to look at these." Willie picked up a pack of cards and read the name on top. "Oooh, Nolan Ryan! I need to get these." Willie picked up another pack and headed for the checkout stand.

"Wait a minute, Willie," his dad said. "I thought you were saving your money."

"I am," Willie said. "I just want to buy these two packs. It's only one dollar. I can earn one extra dollar." Willie went on to pay for the cards as Mr. Teller shook his head.

Later that week, at the kitchen sink, Mr. Teller handed Willie the dishcloth. "Very good, Willie," he said. "You've helped with the dishes every night this week." He dried his hands on a towel before reaching for his wallet. "Here's the money you earned. Tomorrow we go back to the store."

"Great!" Willie's eyes gleamed. "With the money Mom paid me for vacuuming, the money Aunt Sandy sent for my birthday, and this, I should have enough for my glove."

In his room, Willie pulled down his doggy bank. He liked it better than a piggy bank because it looked like his dog, Coco. He popped out the rubber plug in its stomach and reached in for the dollar bills. Coco, who was following him around like always, looked up and whined.

"Aren't you glad I don't do this to you?" Willie said.

"*Warf!*" Coco barked.

Willie counted the dollar bills carefully. He set aside the money he planned to give as tithe. "Wait a minute, I'm missing one dollar. Where is it?" he said to Coco. Then he remembered. He had changed that dollar for four quarters to spend on that video game at the pizza place last night.

Well, he thought, *I only need one more dollar. I know! I'll take some of my baseball cards to school tomorrow and see if I can sell them to Tony or Jason.* Willie reached down to pat Coco's head. "Good idea. Right, Coco?"

"*Warf!*"

The next night, Willie held that beautiful baseball glove in his hands again. "Look, Dad. It's still here, and it still fits perfectly," he said with a big smile.

"Great, son. Let's go get it."

49

Now Willie's smile turned down at the corners. "Well, Dad, I don't have exactly all the money, but . . ."

"What? Even after you spent that dollar on baseball cards, you should still have enough."

Willie's smile fell all the way to a frown. "I spent one dollar at the pizza place playing that video game."

"Willie." Mr. Teller sounded quite disappointed.

But Willie went on. "Then I was going to sell a few baseball cards to my friends today to make the last dollar. But Tony had a great Barry Bonds card and . . ."

"And?"

"I spent another dollar. Now I still need two dollars to buy the glove. Dad, please may I borrow the money from you? Just until I earn two more dollars?"

Mr. Teller looked at Willie. "We agreed last week that you would pay for this glove with your money. You did a good job of working and earning the money. But you didn't make wise decisions about spending it."

Willie swallowed hard. "You mean I can't get the glove tonight?"

"You can get the glove as soon as you can earn and save the money it costs. I could give you the money, but then you wouldn't be learning to make wise decisions about money. And I think that's more important than a baseball glove."

They were nearly home before Willie felt like talking. "Dad, the glove won't be on sale next time. How long will it take to earn enough money now?"

"I think you can have it in two weeks if you keep working hard. And . . ."

Willie finished the sentence for him. "And if I don't spend my money on other things. Don't worry. I've learned my lesson. I'll train Coco to attack if I open my doggy bank."

They both laughed, and Willie felt better. He looked up and saw his face in the car's rearview mirror. He laughed again. "I guess I don't look much like King Solomon this week."

"What?" His dad was confused. Willie explained about "Jesus' Mirror" in the Primary Shoebox.

"And this week our lesson is about King Solomon and how he asked for wisdom. I guess I don't have much wisdom yet."

"But," his dad said, "you look more like Solomon today than you did yesterday. I think you are learning a lot about making wise choices. By the time you buy that glove, you may look like Solomon's twin brother."

By the time they got home, Willie decided that two weeks wasn't such a long time to wait. Not for Solomon's twin brother, anyway.

QUESTIONS

1. Why was the way Willie spent his money not wise?

2. Do you have trouble saving money like Willie did?

3. What other things besides money do you need to be wise about?

4. Have you asked God to give you wisdom? He promises to give it to you!

SOLOMON BUILDS A HOUSE FOR GOD
Give What You Have

When Solomon was a boy, he watched as his father, King David, sent his workers to gather stones and wood to build a temple, a house for God. David wanted to build a special house for God's ark, bigger and better than the palace he built for himself.

But God told him that he couldn't build the temple. "You are a soldier, a man of war," God said to David. "My temple will be built by a man of peace. Your son Solomon will build my temple."

David was sad that he couldn't build the temple, but he did what he could. God gave him the plans for how the temple should be built. So David hired many workers to cut the stones and the wood it would take to build God's temple. They worked for years cutting the stone into perfect blocks. Giant logs of cedar wood were shipped in from faraway places. The men worked hard to get everything ready for when Solomon said to begin.

David gave many pounds of gold and silver to be used in making the temple beautiful. He asked the Israelites to give also, and they gave jewels, silver, bronze, and iron.

Before David died, he gave Solomon the plans that God had given him. Solomon saw that there were plans for a very holy place where God's ark would be kept. He also saw the special work the priests would do in the temple.

Finally it was time to begin. Solomon hired 70,000 workers to carry and put together the building stones and wood. He hired men who knew how to make things beautiful with gold and silver. He hired women to weave beautiful cloths and curtains. He also hired people to make things out of iron and brass.

It took more than 80,000 stone cutters to cut all the stones that were needed. But when it was finished, the temple was beautiful.

Solomon dedicated the temple to God during a long celebration. People came from all over Israel and from many other countries. Solomon led the way as the priests carefully carried the ark to the temple. There was much singing and music along the way.

Solomon built the most beautiful temple he knew how to build. He made it a place where people could worship God and remember how much He had done for them. Solomon's work on the temple was his gift to God.

Give What You Have

"**A**aaah!"

Splaaash!

Jenny heard both noises at the same time. She ran to

the kitchen, holding the shoe she was just about to put on. "Mom?"

Jenny's mom was just standing there, holding an empty pitcher in one hand and an empty glass in the other, staring at the floor. The floor was covered with orange juice. So was the front of her dress.

"What happened?" Jenny asked.

"I was pouring orange juice here at the table, and I guess I poured too fast because the glass fell over. When I tried to grab it, I tipped the pitcher and poured juice everywhere. What a mess! Now I'll have to change these clothes, and we'll be late to Sabbath School."

"Go and change," Jenny said as she laughed. "I'll get the mop and clean this up." Mrs. Wallace hugged Jenny, very carefully so she wouldn't get orange juice on her, then hurried off to change. Jenny got busy with the mop.

Thanks to Jenny, they arrived at the church a few minutes early. "Good morning, Mrs. Shue," Jenny said as she opened the door to the Shoebox.

"Happy Sabbath, Jenny," Mrs. Shue said as she unfolded the chairs. Jenny picked up a stack of songbooks and began placing one on each chair. "How are you this morning, Jenny?"

"I'm fine," Jenny started to say, "but you should have seen what my mother did . . ."

Just then, the door flew open, and Maria and Chris rushed in. Right behind them, Sammy and Willie raced to the corner by the window. Then DeeDee stepped in and quietly closed the door behind her. The Shoebox Kids were ready for Sabbath School.

"Sorry," Mrs. Shue whispered to Jenny. "Tell me after church, OK?"

"Mrs. Shue?" Willie spoke out. "I saw myself in Jesus' Mirror this week." Jenny listened while Willie told about making choices that weren't wise and about not being able to buy his baseball glove.

"But I'm learning," he told his Shoebox friends, "and becoming wiser. I'm looking more like Solomon every day."

"Very good, Willie," Mrs. Shue said. "This week, we are learning more from the life of Solomon. God blessed Solomon with wisdom and with riches. Solomon may have been the richest man in the world. But Solomon wasn't greedy or selfish. He wanted to give gifts back to God for all His blessings. So Solomon had a beautiful temple built."

"Like our church?" Chris asked.

"Yes, it was a place to worship God like our church. But it was much, much bigger. Solomon gave tons of gold to make it the most beautiful building on earth." Mrs. Shue held up a picture of Solomon's temple. "This is what we think it looked like on the outside."

"Ooooh!"

"It was beautiful!"

Mrs. Shue gave everyone a chance to see it up close. Then she went on. "What we can learn from Solomon this week is that giving gifts to God does something for us. It will make us happy."

"But we don't have tons of gold. I don't even have tons of pennies!" Chris said with a laugh.

Mrs. Shue laughed too. "None of us have as much money as Solomon did. But there are things we can give

God besides money. Can you think of any other things that people give God?"

"Last week, Pastor Hill said that when he decided to be a preacher, he wanted to give his voice to God," Sammy said. "So every time he preaches, he is giving a gift to God."

DeeDee raised her hand. "My piano teacher says that learning to play the piano is developing a talent God has given you. Then when you play a song, it is like giving a gift back to God."

"That's right, DeeDee," Mrs. Shue said. "Anyone who can play an instrument or sing a song can give gifts of music to God. What other kind of gifts can we give?"

Willie spoke up. "When we took some clothes and food to a poor family at Christmas, my mother said we were giving our Christmas present to Jesus. So I guess giving to help others is like giving to God."

"Jesus taught us that, Willie," Mrs. Shue agreed. "He said, 'Whatever you do for someone in need, you do it for Me.' There are many kinds of gifts we can give. Solomon gave great riches because that is what he had. All we have to do is give what we have."

Jenny didn't say anything, but she thought to herself, *I'm not sure I have anything to give.*

Later, when Jenny sat by her mother in church, she was still thinking about what she could give to God. She was trying to listen to Pastor Hill's sermon in case he talked about giving gifts, when she heard little Elisabeth Dooley in the row across from them.

"Mama! Mama, look, look!"

Mrs. Dooley looked embarrassed. "Whisper, Elisabeth. We whisper in church." Jenny watched as Elisabeth sat quietly for a minute, drawing on a sheet on paper. When she was done, she got up to show her mother again.

"Mama, look!" Elisabeth whispered, but her whisper was louder than her talking.

Jenny leaned toward her mother and whispered quietly. "May I go sit by Elisabeth?" Her mother looked over as Mrs. Dooley tried to keep both her new baby and Elisabeth quiet. She nodded to Jenny.

Jenny slipped into the row by Elisabeth. "Hi!" she whispered. "Want to show me your pictures?" Mrs. Dooley smiled at her, and Jenny sat with them until the last song.

When church was over, she waited for her mother at their car. Mrs. Shue walked by carrying some bags, and Jenny ran to help her. "Thank you, Jenny. You were going to tell me something after church today, weren't you?" Mrs. Shue asked.

Jenny smiled. "I was going to tell you about my mother's orange juice bath this morning." She told the story, and they both laughed. "But Mrs. Shue, I've been thinking about giving gifts to God, and I don't think I have any to give. I can't play the piano like DeeDee or preach like Pastor Hill. I haven't gone out to give things to poor people like Willie did. I don't have anything to give God."

Mrs. Shue burst out laughing again. "Oh, Jenny. Think about what you have done just this morning. You helped your mother with her orange-juice disaster. You helped me get ready for Sabbath School. You helped Mrs. Dooley

in church. Yes, I saw you sit by Elisabeth. And now, you've helped me carry these bags to the car. You've spent all morning helping people."

"But I wanted to do those things. I wanted to help. That's not giving a gift to God, is it?"

"That's exactly what it is. God gave you the gift of helping others, and every time you use it, you are giving a gift back to Him. And giving to others makes you the happy person that you are. I think you like to give gifts as much as Solomon did."

Jenny smiled. "Maybe I do look a little bit like Solomon."

Mrs. Shue hugged her. "In Jesus' Mirror, you look a lot like him."

QUESTIONS

1. Can you think of other gifts that people give to God?

2. Did you know that every time you help someone else, you are giving a gift? It's called the gift of service!

3. What gifts have you given to God this week?

4. Does giving gifts of service make you happy? Try it this week and see if it does.

7

CHAPTER

GOD DOES IMPOSSIBLE THINGS FOR ELIJAH

Runaway Herman

King Solomon ruled Israel for many years. But after he died, the kingdom split into two parts: Judah and Israel. Jerusalem was the capital city of Judah. The people of Israel built a new capital and a new palace for their king in Samaria. As the years went by, many people in Israel began to worship idols.

About seventy years after Solomon, King Ahab began to rule Israel. He worshiped idols instead of following God. He even built an altar to the false god Baal right in Samaria. His wife, Jezebel, didn't even believe in God. She taught many of the Israelites to worship her false gods and idols.

Elijah was a prophet in Israel in those days. He tried to teach the people to worship God. He begged them to stay away from idols. But they wouldn't listen. Elijah cried out to God, "Your people are making a big mistake and sinning. Do something to make them listen and change their minds!"

So God gave Elijah a special message to take to King

Ahab. Elijah walked day and night until he got to the palace in Samaria. Then he walked right through the gates, right through the halls, and right up to Ahab's throne. As everyone in the room stared, he pointed to heaven. "There will be no more rain or dew on the grass in this land until I command it to happen. These words are true, just as it is true that God is alive."

King Ahab was so surprised that he just sat there. Before he could do anything, Elijah walked out and disappeared. But Elijah knew the king would be looking for him. "Where should I go to hide?" he asked God.

God had a plan. "Go to the little brook called Cherith on the other side of the Jordan River. You can drink water from the brook, and I will send ravens to you with food."

So Elijah hid by the little brook. Every morning and evening, the ravens brought him bits of bread and meat. But just as Elijah had promised the king, it did not rain even once. After a few months, the water in the brook dried up.

God told Elijah, "Go to the village of Zarephath. A widow there will feed you." (A widow is a woman whose husband has died.)

So Elijah walked to Zarephath. When he got there, he saw a woman gathering sticks by the road. "Would you bring me some water in a cup?" he asked the woman. "I'm thirsty." As she turned away to get the water, he said, "Please bring me a piece of bread too."

The woman shook her head sadly. "I have no bread. All I have is a little flour left in a pot and a little oil left in a jar. I'm gathering these sticks to build a fire and bake one last little loaf of bread for my child and me. Then we will starve."

Elijah smiled. "Don't worry. Make me some bread first. Then cook something for yourself and your son. God has told me: 'Your pot of flour will never be empty, and your jar will never run out of oil until it rains again.' "

The woman went home and did just what Elijah said. She poured a little flour out of her pot and then a little oil from her jar. Then she mixed it up and baked a small loaf of bread for Elijah. Then she went back to her house and tipped the pot again. A little flour came out! Then she tipped up the jar of oil. A little oil came out!

The woman made a loaf of bread for herself and her son. Then she invited Elijah to stay in her home. And there was always just enough flour and oil to make bread every day.

Later, the woman's son got sick. She took care of him, but he got weaker and weaker until he died. She cried to Elijah, "Why did you do this to me? Did God send you to punish me?"

Elijah was sad too. "Give me your son," he said. Then he took the boy upstairs to his room and laid him on the bed. He prayed, "Lord, this widow let me stay in her house. Lord, let this boy live again!"

Elijah prayed three times. Then the boy started to breathe again! He was alive!

Elijah quickly carried the boy back downstairs to his mother. "Look!" he cried. "Your son is alive again!"

Because Elijah was faithful, God took care of him. Over and over, God did impossible things for his prophet Elijah.

Runaway Herman

"Chris, don't forget to clean out your hamster's cage."

"OK, Mom." Chris put his school things away and went over to his pet's cage. "Hello," he said to the little brown-and-white ball of fur. "How is my friend Herman?"

Herman the Hamster just stared at Chris with his two beady black eyes. Then he crossed over to the glass, stood up on his back legs, and reached up toward Chris.

"Oh, are you hungry, Herman?" Herman always stood on his back legs to beg for food. "How about some yummy hamster food while I clean your cage?" Chris picked Herman up and placed him in an empty shoebox. "Look, Herman. Now you can be a Shoebox Kid too!"

While he grabbed the food, Chris worried a little about the size of the shoebox. Herman could probably climb out if he tried hard. *Well,* he thought, *I'll give him plenty of food. He'll be too busy eating to try to climb out.*

With Herman safely crunching on his food, Chris got busy emptying the old shredded bark from the cage. He also cleaned and refilled the water jug. "You'll really like your cage now, Herman," Chris said out loud. "Are you ready to go home?"

Herman didn't answer. Chris didn't expect him to, of course, but he did expect to hear something. He expected to hear Herman crunching on his food. But it was very quiet in the shoebox. Chris rushed over and looked in.

"Herman?" But the box was empty.

Quickly, Chris got down on the floor and looked under the bed. No Herman. He looked under the dresser. Still no Herman. He was crawling toward the door when his mother walked in.

"Chris, why are you crawling around on the floor?"

Chris didn't want to tell her that Herman had escaped, but he needed help. "It's Herman. He got away while I was cleaning his cage. Help me look for him, please."

"A hamster loose in my house! Chris, what happened? Never mind, we'll talk about it later. Now, where did you see him last?" Mrs. Vargas got down on her knees, too, and looked under the desk. "Did you look under your dresser?"

"Yes, Mom." But he looked again anyway. The bottom drawer was open just a little. Chris snatched it all the way open, but he saw nothing except his good sweaters. He closed it.

Thirty minutes later, they gave up. "We've looked everywhere in this room," Mrs. Vargas said, "and in the hall and in your sister's room. I guess all we can do is watch and wait."

Chris's chin dropped down onto his hands. He really liked Herman. "What if we never find him? What if he leaves the house and never comes back?"

"He won't leave, Chris. He doesn't have anywhere to go. The only home he knows is his cage."

Chris thought about that. "Wait," he said, "I have a

plan. I'll put his cage on the floor, leave the door open, and put food inside. Then we'll leave, and when it's nice and quiet, he'll come back to his cage to eat. Herman loves to eat."

Later, Chris crept quietly up to the door of his room. He could see the cage on the floor where he left it. But with the light turned off, he couldn't see if Herman was back home. He held his breath and snapped on the switch. The cage was empty.

The next morning, at the Shoebox, Chris told his friends that Herman was still missing. "Now I'm worried that he's going to starve."

"Did you look in your pillowcase?" Jenny asked.

Everyone turned and looked at her. "What?" Maria asked.

Jenny's face turned red. "Once I couldn't find my cat, and she was hiding in my pillowcase."

Everyone laughed. Maria said, "You must have found her before you went to sleep. Anyway, we searched everywhere a hamster could go in Chris's room and in my room. But Herman wasn't there."

Chris smiled at his sister. "Mrs. Shue, is it all right to pray that Herman is safe and that he will come back?"

Mrs. Shue smiled. "It's always all right to pray, Chris. God cares about you and everything in your life, even Herman. I'm sure He is pleased that you take good care of Herman. God loves to take care of His friends."

Chris smiled and felt a little better. *If God worries about me as much as I'm worried about Herman, He really does care what happens to me,* he thought.

"We've talked about caring for animals this morning," Mrs. Shue said to the class, "but our lesson tells about animals that cared for a person. God used ravens to bring food to Elijah when he was hiding from King Ahab."

"It must have been hard for Elijah to believe that God could send him food like that," said DeeDee.

"It must have been hard for Elijah to eat food that birds carried in their beaks," said Jenny. Everyone laughed again. "Well, it was probably dirty."

Mrs. Shue laughed too. "Well, don't forget that God had stopped the rain in the land and many people didn't have enough food. Elijah was probably glad for whatever food he could get."

"Ms. Shue?" Chris had his hand raised. "I think I know what would be the hardest thing. I think the hardest thing is to believe that God really does want to take care of you. Just like I want to take care of Herman."

"You're right, Chris. If your hamster could really understand that you will take care of him and feed him, he would run right back to you. Sometimes, people forget how much Jesus cares, and they stop following Him. We all need to learn what Elijah was learning by the brook. That God loves to take care of us—and that He will take care of us, no matter what happens."

That night, Chris's family was getting ready to go to a party. "Chris, wear your heavy sweater, it's cold out tonight," Mrs. Vargas called from her room.

"OK, Mom," Chris answered. He grabbed a sweater from his drawer and pulled it over his head. When everyone was finally ready, he started out the door.

"Wait!" Mrs. Vargas grabbed at Chris's arm. She pointed at his back. "What did you do to your sweater?"

"What?" asked Chris, twisting his neck to try to see.

"This big hole. It's ripped open. No," she looked closer, "it's been cut. Who cut your sweater?"

Chris looked puzzled. "I haven't worn this sweater since Christmas. How could it get cut in my dresser drawer?" He pulled the sweater over his head. "It looks like it was cut by . . . wait a minute!" Chris turned and ran down the hall.

"Chris, where are you going?"

"Ah ha! I knew it!" Chris walked back with Herman in his hands.

"Herman!" Maria squealed. "Where did you find him?"

"He was in the sweater drawer. He's the one who ate my sweater. He must have crawled in under the sweaters where I couldn't see him. When I shut the drawer, he couldn't get out."

When Herman was safely back in his cage, crunching his food, Chris and his family went to the party. Sitting in the back seat, Chris said a prayer.

"Thank You, God, for keeping Herman safe. Thank You for helping me learn how much You care about me. Thank You for teaching me the same things You taught Elijah."

QUESTIONS
1. Did you guess where Herman was?
2. Do you have a pet that you care about like Chris did?
3. Have you learned the lesson Elijah was learning?
4. Did you know that God loves to care about you?

CHAPTER

FIRE ON THE MOUNTAIN
Stand Up at the Swings

"You are the biggest troublemaker in Israel!"

When King Ahab finally saw Elijah again after three long, dry, dusty years, he was very angry.

Elijah had been hiding in Zarephath when God sent him back to King Ahab with a message. "Don't blame this drought on me," Elijah told the king. "You caused it by following the false god, Baal."

Elijah delivered God's message. "Come to Mount Carmel. Bring your prophets of Baal and invite all who want to see which god is stronger."

A big crowd followed Elijah, King Ahab, and the priests up the mountain. At the top, Elijah spoke to the people. "How long have you been trying to follow Baal and God? You can't do both. Let's have a contest. If Baal is stronger, we'll worship him. But if God is the strongest, we'll follow only Him.

"This will be the contest. The priests of Baal will make a sacrifice on their altar. I will make one on my altar. We will each pray. The god who answers with fire from heaven is the true God!"

The priests of Baal went first. They put wood and a sacrifice on their altar. They called out to Baal. They shouted, jumped, and danced. But nothing happened.

Elijah made fun of them. "Pray louder! Maybe Baal is off on a trip, and he can't hear you. Maybe he is asleep—shout louder so you can wake him up!"

The priests continued to shout all day, but no fire came down from heaven.

Finally, it was Elijah's turn. He picked up stones that had once been an altar to God and stacked them up again. Then he dug a ditch around this altar. Next he stacked wood on the top, and then the sacrifice. But he didn't stop there. He had some men haul four barrels of water and dump them on the altar.

"Do it again," he told them. "And again," he said. By now, the altar, the wood, and the sacrifice were soaked. Even the ditch around the altar was filled with water.

Then Elijah prayed. "Lord, show these people that You are the true God, the only God. Then they will know that You are reaching out to bring them back to You."

Almost before the words were out of Elijah's mouth, fire flashed down from heaven! It burned the sacrifice. It burned the wood. It burned the altar stones. It even burned the water in the ditch!

When the people saw the fire, they fell down and cried out, "Elijah's God is the true God!"

Now that the people had seen God's power, Elijah prayed seven times for rain. A single black cloud appeared. Elijah said, "Tell King Ahab to hurry back to his palace. A real storm is coming." Then he ran all the way down the mountain in front of the king's chariot, all the way to the palace.

When Queen Jezebel heard what had happened, she was furious! She said, "Elijah, before tomorrow is over, I will have you killed."

Eliajh was very tired. When he heard Jezebel say that, he ran for his life. God was disappointed that Elijah forgot to trust Him, but He still took care of His friend.

When Elijah was finally too tired to run any farther, he lay down under a tree to sleep. Suddenly, he felt someone touching him. Elijah's eyes popped open. It was an angel! "Wake up and eat," the angel said, pointing to a plate of food fixed just for Elijah.

Elijah ate the food and fell asleep again.

"Wake up and eat!" The angel touched Elijah again after he had slept. Another meal was waiting. This time, Elijah ate and then walked all the way to Mt. Sinai. He hid there in a cave. "Elijah, what are you doing here?" God asked.

"I'm the only one left who truly believes in You," Elijah answered. "They want to kill me."

"Go stand at the top of the mountain," God said. Elijah climbed up and waited. Before long, a terrible wind began to blow. Rocks were flying through the air and smashing against one another! Elijah ducked and held on. But God did not speak to Elijah from the wind. Finally, it stopped blowing.

Then the ground started to shake. It was an earthquake! Boulders as big as houses tumbled down the mountain. Elijah was afraid he would tumble down next. But God did not speak through the earthquake. Finally, it stopped shaking.

Then, farther down the mountain, Elijah heard a crackling sound. It was a fire! The flames burned higher than any fire Elijah had ever seen. He bowed down to escape the heat. But God did not speak from the fire. Finally, the fire went out.

Elijah waited. Then he heard it. It was a soft whisper of a voice. "Elijah, what are you doing here?" God asked.

"I'm the only one left who truly believes in you," Elijah answered. "They want to kill me."

"Go back to our people," God said. "Choose Elisha to be your successor. He will stay with you everywhere you go and will be the next prophet when you are gone."

So Elijah returned. With his new friend, Elisha, he continued to do God's work. Even when it was danger- ous, Elijah stood up for God. God protected Elijah from the king and the drought. He protected Elijah from the angry queen, even when Elijah was tired and afraid.

Stand Up at the Swings

"I wish I could have been there," DeeDee said. "Stand- ing up for God at the top of the mountain like Elijah did would have been exciting."

"But wouldn't you have been afraid?" Maria asked. "I mean, all those priests were against him. And the people weren't with him either. They were just watching."

"But Elijah knew he was doing what God wanted him to do. He didn't care what the people or the priests thought. He didn't have anything to be afraid of. He was standing up for God."

"I'm sure that standing up for God and praying for fire to come down from heaven was one of the most exciting things Elijah ever did," Mrs. Shue agreed. "But it wasn't an easy thing. Sometimes, it's not easy to stand up and do the right thing even when you know that God would want you to."

Well, I think it would be great to stand up for God like that, DeeDee said to herself.

The next week in school, DeeDee put away her math book and waited for the teacher to announce the morning recess. Suddenly, a folded piece of paper dropped on her desk.

"Read it!" she heard her friend, Kim, whisper. DeeDee opened the note and read:

DeeDee

Let's run straight to the swings and grab them before anyone else does.

Kim

DeeDee turned and nodded to her friend. By running as soon as they were out the door, they got into the swings first. Leaning way back, they kicked their feet and started swinging, side-by-side.

"Hey, we were going to swing," Angela said as she and Sandy ran up.

"Well, we got here first, so too bad," Kim said as she swung down past the two girls.

"You'll just have to wait your turn," DeeDee added. Since there were only two swings, the rule was that a person could swing for only five minutes. Then they had to let someone else take a turn, if someone was waiting.

"Come on, Sandy. We'll wait over there by the monkey bars," Angela said. "I'm counting the minutes," she shouted back at DeeDee and Kim, pointing to her watch.

By then, Kim and DeeDee were zooming into the sky, almost even with the top bar of the swingset. "I love to swing," shouted Kim as they dropped back toward the ground.

After a few minutes went by, they stopped pumping and began to slow down and coast to a stop. Their five minutes were running out. "Wait," Kim said as DeeDee started to jump out of the swing. "Look. Angela and Sandy are watching the baseball game. They're not paying attention."

"I'll call them," DeeDee said, jumping out of her swing.

"No, wait. The rule says that you can swing only five minutes if someone else is waiting. OK," Kim added, stepping out of her swing, "we stopped. No one is waiting to swing, so we can take another turn."

"But," DeeDee looked over at Angela, who was still watching the baseball players, "we know they wanted a turn next."

"It's fair," Kim argued. "They aren't here waiting. Let's go." She jumped back into her swing and started pumping, so DeeDee sat back in hers, too. "Start swinging, quick before they turn around," Kim whispered.

DeeDee leaned back and started swinging. "It might be fair," she said, "but it's not very nice."

"Hey, it's our turn." Angela had finally turned around. "Your five minutes are over."

"We stopped when our five minutes were over," Kim laughed as she went by, "but no one was here waiting to swing, so we're taking another turn."

"That's not fair. You and DeeDee are cheating. I'm telling Mrs. Peterson." Angela turned and ran toward the teacher. Sandy stuck her tongue out at them before she turned and ran too.

DeeDee just kept swinging. She didn't look at anyone or say anything.

"Brats!" Kim yelled. "I guess we showed them something," she said to DeeDee.

DeeDee watched Angela tell her story to Mrs. Peterson. She couldn't hear anything, but she saw that her friend Maria was listening, too. Suddenly she didn't want to swing anymore. She dragged her feet in the sand. "I'm getting off," she said.

Kim stopped too. "Good idea. That way, we can't get in trouble with Mrs. Peterson. Let's go over to the drinking fountain."

After a few more minutes, recess was over, and DeeDee was back in her desk. She tried to smile at Sandy on her way to the pencil sharpener, but Sandy turned away and ignored her. *I don't like how this feels,* DeeDee said to herself. *I'm used to being friends with Sandy and Angela and everyone.*

Just before the afternoon recess, another note dropped on her desk. She unfolded it.

DeeDee

Let's grab the swings again. Try to be first in line for recess.

Kim

DeeDee shook her head. "I don't want to swing anymore," she whispered to Kim.

"Hey, I want to show Angela and Sandy that they can't tell us what to do. We'll just swing for five minutes and then leave." Kim whispered back.

DeeDee shook her head again. Kim frowned. "I can't keep them off the swings by myself. Are you my friend or not?"

DeeDee nodded her head slowly. She joined Kim at the front of the line and raced with her to the swings. They jumped on just before Angela and Sandy got there.

"Hey, no fair! We didn't even get to swing last recess," Angela shouted at them.

"Too bad," Kim shouted back, swinging hard. DeeDee stared at her feet and moved her swing just a little.

"I hate you both," Sandy shouted. "You're selfish and mean."

DeeDee felt her eyes feel with tears. "Wait," she said, hopping down from her swing. "You're right. I'm sorry. It should be your turn." Then she turned and ran back to the school, ignoring Kim's shouts to her. She ran into the classroom and put her head on her desk.

After a minute, she heard someone come in. Then she heard Maria's voice. "Are you OK, DeeDee?"

DeeDee raised her head and wiped her eyes. "I guess I didn't act much like Elijah today. Standing up for what's right is harder than I thought."

Maria just smiled at her. "Let's go get a drink before recess is over."

QUESTIONS

1. Have you ever wished that you could have been on the mountaintop with Elijah?

2. What should DeeDee have done?

3. What should DeeDee have said to Kim?

4. Can you think of a time when someone talked you into doing the wrong thing?

5. Did you know that God is always there to help you do the right thing?

CHAPTER

HORSES MADE OF FIRE
Elijah's Picnic

Elijah followed God's directions. He walked to a field where Elisha was plowing. He took off his big coat and put it on Elisha. This meant that God had chosen Elisha to be a prophet like Elijah.

Elisha left his plow in the field and went straight to his house. He told his mother and father goodbye, and then he followed Elijah away.

Elisha learned many things from Elijah as they walked around the country together. They spoke to people about God and His plan for them. They visited the schools of the prophets where young men were learning to follow God and teach others.

Finally, it was time for Elijah's work to end. "I must go now," Elijah said as they left one of the schools. "You can stay here."

"I won't leave you," Elisha answered. "I want to go with you." And so he did.

At the next school, Elijah said again, "Elisha, stay here. I must go on to the Jordan River."

Elisha shook his head again. "I won't leave you," he said. And he stayed with Elijah. When they reached the river, Elijah took off his coat. He rolled it up and hit the water with it. The water rolled back on both sides, and the two of them walked across to the other side on dry ground!

Then Elijah asked, "What can I do for you before I go?"

Elisha wanted only one thing. "Give me the power you have to be God's prophet."

Elijah smiled. "If you are with me when I am taken away, you will get what you ask for." And they walked on beside the river.

Suddenly, there was a loud noise. A chariot made of fire pulled by horses made of fire rushed right between Elijah and Elisha. This was a chariot sent from heaven to pick up Elijah!

"My father!" Elisha called out as Elijah flew up into the sky on the chariot in a whirlwind of fire. Then Elijah was gone. But his big coat fell out of the sky, and Elisha picked it up. Now he knew for sure that God had chosen him to carry on Elijah's work.

Elijah was God's faithful prophet, and God did something amazing for him. He took Elijah, who never died, straight to heaven to live with Him.

Elijah's Picnic

"Do I have to go?" Sammy asked, as his grandmother searched through his closet for his white shirt.

"Yes, Sammy. You have to go with us. We can't leave you at home alone, and you have no one else to stay with."

Sammy frowned, but he knew his grandmother was right. Willie and his family had company that day, and Chris's family was gone somewhere because no one had answered their phone.

"I know you don't really want to go, Sammy, but I think you'll have a good time. All the families from your grandfather's work will be there. There are sure to be many children. Bring along your baseball glove. Maybe they'll want to play a game."

Maybe, Sammy thought, *but I don't know if I'll want to. I won't know any of them.* He got dressed, but he still wasn't happy about going. A company picnic sounded like fun unless you were going to be there alone with no friends.

On the way, Sammy's grandmother spoke up. "Sammy, I want to tell you a story. Remember when you first moved to this town?"

Sammy thought back. It was only two years ago that he had moved in with his grandparents. "Yes, I remember."

"Remember how unhappy you were when you arrived? You had no friends, and you said that the kids here were unfriendly."

Sammy remembered. He hadn't made any friends that first summer. He had hated Mill Valley. "But it's not that way now," he protested. "I like it here in Mill Valley."

"Why?"

"I like my school and my friends here. I like my Shoebox friends at Sabbath School."

"Do you see the difference? You like it here now because you made friends. You got to know people. Well, tonight you have the chance to make new friends. The children there will be friendly if you are."

Sammy thought about that the rest of the way to the park where the picnic was being held. Maybe his grandmother was right. Maybe he could have fun tonight if he tried to make new friends. By the time they arrived, Sammy had decided to try to be friendly.

After helping his grandmother carry their folding chairs to the picnic area, Sammy looked around and took a deep breath. "See you later, Grandmother," he said as he picked up his glove. She smiled at him as he walked toward the playground where several other kids were already running and shouting.

Sammy stopped by a tree that was next to the swings. Two girls were swinging as high as they could. Four little kids were screaming up and down the slide. Three boys about his age were playing catch. Sammy put his hand in his glove and pounded on it with his fist. He was waiting for them to ask him to join them.

"No," he whispered to himself. "I said I was going to make friends, and I am going to try." He walked out to where they were playing.

"Hey, you want to play?" one of the kids called to him.

Sammy nodded his head, kind of surprised. "Yes."

"Great! Let's play 500-Up. Seth, you bat first. Me and Carter and . . . what's your name?"

"Sammy," Sammy said.

"I'm E.J. We'll be out first." E.J. explained the way they

84

kept points in 500-Up. "You get a hundred points for catching a fly, fifty points for a bouncer, and twenty-five for a roller. Whoever gets to five hundred first goes in to bat. OK, Seth, hit one!"

Seth hit one. It went up, up, up, right toward Sammy. He stepped back two steps, and pop—it landed in his glove!

"Good catch," Carter yelled as Sammy tossed it back in. "That's a hundred."

As the game went on, Sammy caught two more, but E.J. reached five hundred first and went in to bat. Several new kids joined the game, but Sammy didn't take time to say Hello. Another fly was heading toward him. It was going higher so he started back. Back, back, back he went until bump, he backed into another kid, and they both fell down. The ball fell right between them.

Sammy rolled over, kind of mad that he had missed the ball, and kind of afraid that the kids would all be mad at him for tripping one of their friends. He looked over at the other kid on the ground.

"Chris!"

"Sammy?"

"What are you doing here?" Sammy jumped up and held out his hand to his friend and pulled him up. "No wonder you weren't home when I called. You were coming to this picnic too."

Chris laughed. "I didn't think I would know anyone here, so I was kind of afraid to play. And then I knocked someone down the first time I tried to catch a fly. I sure am glad it was you."

"Hey," someone yelled, "throw the ball back in."

"These guys are friendly," Sammy said as he tossed the ball back to E.J. "That's E.J. batting, and that's Carter, and that's Seth."

"You sure do make friends quickly, Sammy," Chris said.

Sammy had to laugh about that.

Later, on the way home, Sammy told his grandmother about the fun he had. "I had fun playing, and those guys were friendly, but it sure was nice to see Chris there."

She turned and looked at Sammy. "I know your lesson this week is about Elijah going to heaven. Did you ever think of why Elijah or anyone would want to go to heaven?"

"Sure," answered Sammy. "Heaven will be great! There will be fun stuff to do and great things to eat."

"But you knew that the picnic today would have good food and that the park would be fun to play in. But you still didn't want to go."

"Yes," Sammy agreed, "but that's because I didn't know anyone, and I thought I wouldn't have any friends."

"So why would heaven be any different?" His grandmother's eyes twinkled as she asked him.

Sammy thought about it. "I guess if you didn't know anyone in heaven, it might be lonely. Wait a minute. Everyone in heaven will have a friend. Jesus will be there."

Grandmother Tan laughed. "That's why Elijah wanted to go to heaven. He already knew Someone there. He knew God was there. That's why all of us will be happy in heaven—because Jesus will be there."

"Maybe Elijah knew that God was planning a picnic that day," Sammy laughed. Then he was quiet for a few minutes. "Maybe that's why some people will choose not to go to heaven. They don't know Jesus, so they don't want to be with Him," he added.

His grandmother nodded her head sadly.

The next Sabbath, Sammy told his Shoebox friends all about the picnic and what he had learned. "So the kind of people who will be in heaven are ones who are friends of Jesus."

Mrs. Shue agreed. "So can you see how we can be getting ready for heaven everyday here on earth?" she asked.

Sammy nodded. "We can get ready by getting to be closer friends with Jesus."

"Sammy," Mrs. Shue said, "everyday you get to be closer friends with Jesus, you look more like Elijah, like someone who wants to go to heaven."

Sammy just nodded his head and smiled.

QUESTIONS

1. Do you ever have to go places with your parent that you don't want to go?

2. What things could you do to make new friends easily?

3. Why do you want to go to heaven?

4. What are you doing to become better friends with Jesus today?

5. Aren't you glad Jesus is coming soon?

CHAPTER 10

THE FAITH OF ELISHA
The Lost Book

One day a woman came to Elisha. "I need help," she said. Her husband had been at one of the schools of the prophets, but he had died. "My husband owed a man some money. Now the man wants to take my sons to be slaves to pay that debt. What can I do?"

Elisha looked at her and her sons. "What do you have in your house?" he asked.

"Only one jar of oil," she said sadly.

Elisha smiled. "Go to all your neighbors and borrow their jars—not just a few, but as many jars as you can. Then go home and shut your door so no one can see. Pour the oil from your jar into each of the borrowed jars until they are full."

So the woman did exactly what Elisha said. She and her sons went to all their neighbors and borrowed as many jars as they could. Then they went home and closed the door. The woman picked up her jar of oil and said, "Hand me an empty jar."

Her sons handed her a jar, and she poured oil into it

until it was full. Then she said, "Hand me another jar." She poured oil into the second jar until it was full. "Bring me another jar," she said. She kept asking until her sons said, "There are no more jars."

The oil poured out of her jar until all the borrowed jars were full! Then it was empty. The woman went to Elisha and told him what had happened. Elisha said, "Go sell the oil and pay what your husband owes. Then you and your sons can live on the money left over."

Whenever Elisha traveled from the schools of the prophets to his home at Mount Carmel, he passed through the village of Shunem. Every time he passed by, a wealthy woman who lived there asked him to stop and eat at her house. One day the woman said to her husband, "Let's build a little room just for Elisha. That way he'll have a comfortable place of his own whenever he comes to our town."

The next time Elisha came to Shunem, he was delighted when he saw what they had done. "What can I do to thank this kind woman?" he asked his servant Gehazi. "Do you think she needs anything?"

Gehazi said, "Well, her husband is getting older, and they don't have a son to care for her after he is gone."

Elisha nodded. "I'm sure she would like to have a son. Call her in here, please."

When the woman came in, Elisha said, "Next year, you will be holding a baby boy."

"Ohhh!" The woman almost fainted. "Please don't say that it if isn't true, Sir. I have wanted a son so badly."

But it was true. The next year when Elisha visited

Shunem, the woman was holding a baby boy. One day when the boy was older, he was out helping his father in the fields on a hot day. Suddenly he cried out, "Oh, my head! My head hurts!"

"Quickly, take him home to his mother," the father said. The servants took him home, and his mother did what she could, but the boy died. Sadly, she placed him on the bed in Elisha's room. Then she and her servant hurried all the way to Elisha's house.

When Elisha heard what happened, he rushed back to the woman's house. He went into the room where the boy was lying and shut the door. Then he prayed and asked God to make the boy live again. God answered Elisha's prayer. The boy sat up and sneezed seven times! He was alive again!

Because of Elisha's faith in God, he was able to do impossible things. God loves to reward people who have faith in Him.

The Lost Book

"**M**aria, it's Friday. Don't forget your library book today," Maria's mother called from the kitchen.

"OK, Mom," Maria answered. But to herself she said, "I remember it. I just don't remember where it is." She sat down on her bed and tried to picture just where the book might be. She had finished reading it last Monday. It should be on her bookshelf. But she had already flipped through the jumbled books there. The missing library book wasn't there.

Maybe it had fallen under her bed. She dropped to her knees and pulled up the bedspread. There was a barrette, one red sock, and some old school papers, but no book. Maybe it was still in her book bag, under her spelling book and English papers. Maria lifted her book bag with a grunt. *It's heavy enough for ten library books,* she thought. But inside she found only school-books and papers.

"Maria, let's go. I don't want to be late." From the sound of her mother's voice, Maria knew that she was in the hall closet, getting everyone's coats and sweaters. *Maybe the library book is in there,* Maria thought.

"Coming, Mother." She snatched up her bag and ran to the hall closet. She stepped in just as her mother was stepping out.

"Maria! Be careful, I almost stepped on you. Here's your sweater. I know it will be warm this afternoon, but this morning, you need a sweater." Maria stood back as her mother passed out sweaters to Chris and her little sister, Yoyo. Then she took a quick look around the closet. No library book.

On the way to school, Maria kept very quiet. She was hoping that her mother would forget to ask about the library book. She was hoping that it might be in her desk at school.

"Maria, did you get your library book?"

Maria sighed. "No, I couldn't find it. I think it might be in my desk at school."

Mrs. Vargas looked sharply at her daughter in the rear-view mirror. "I hope it is. You know that if there are any fines for bringing a library book back late, you have to pay for them out of your own money."

"I know, I know."

The book wasn't in Maria's desk. At library time, she explained her problem to Mrs. Peterson. "I don't know where it is. I'll probably have to pay for a new one."

"Let's not say that yet," Mrs. Peterson said. "There won't even be a fine until Monday. You have all weekend to look for the book. I'm sure you can find it. Have you asked Jesus to help you remember where you put it?"

"No," Maria admitted.

"Don't forget to do that. Jesus cares about even the little things in our lives. Even our lost library books."

"OK," Maria said. But inside, she wasn't sure that Jesus would help her find a book that she shouldn't have lost.

That afternoon, Mrs. Vargas was unhappy to hear that the book was still lost. "Well, it's a good reason for you to clean your room from top to bottom. Straighten out that bookshelf, make your bed, put away your toys, and you might be surprised to find the book right in front of your nose."

For once, Maria liked the idea of cleaning her room. She got so carried away cleaning that she forgot all about the book. When everything was in its place, she stopped and looked around, pleased that it all looked so nice. Then she remembered that the library book hadn't turned up.

"We'll have to look through the rest of the house," her mother said. So Maria searched through the bookshelves in Chris's room and in Yoyo's room. She looked under their beds and in their closets. Then she searched the living room too.

"It's just not here, Mom," she reported at bedtime.

"Have you asked Jesus to help you find it?" her mother asked.

"No," Maria admitted. "I didn't know if I should since it's my fault that the book is lost."

Her mother squeezed her tight. "Maria, it's always all right to ask for Jesus' help. Even if we cause the problem ourselves, He still wants to help us. He loves to answer our prayers."

Maria prayed before she went to sleep. "Jesus, I'm sorry I lost my book. Please help me find it before Monday."

The next morning, Maria didn't see the book as she got ready for Sabbath School. She didn't really look for it, since she had looked everywhere the day before.

At the Shoebox, the lesson was about Elisha and the wonderful things he did for God. "Elisha had faith that God heard his prayers. And since he had great faith, God was able to use him to do great things," Mrs. Shue said. Maria raised her hand.

"Mrs. Shue, should I have faith that God will help me with a problem that's my fault?" She told them about the library book. Everyone nodded their heads and listened for Mrs. Shue's answer. They were used to losing library books and things and looking for them.

"I lose things, too," Mrs. Shue said, "so I know that God's promises aren't just for people who don't make mistakes. His promises are for anyone who has faith, anyone who believes that He can and will help them. He doesn't always give us what we ask for, but He always gives us what is best for us."

"So God will help me?" Maria asked.

"God loves to reward us when we have faith in Him, just like He rewarded Elisha. In Jesus' Mirror, Maria, you look just like Elisha when you have faith."

Before she left the Shoebox, Maria prayed, "Jesus, I believe that You will help me just like You helped Elisha. Help me to have faith to believe that You will do what is best for me."

By bedtime that evening, Maria was tempted to give up believing that she would find the library book. But she didn't. She looked in the car and was searching her dad's bookshelves, when her mother called.

"Maria, would you put Yoyo in bed and read her a story?"

Maria wanted to say she was busy looking for her book, but she really had nowhere else to look. "OK."

By the time she finished reading Yoyo's story and was tucking her in bed, Maria decided that she didn't feel bad about the missing book. *It will be OK*, she decided, *even if I don't find the book before school tomorrow.*

"Hey," she said to Yoyo, "what is this doll doing in your bed?" Yoyo just giggled. Maria reached farther back under the covers. "And what about this plastic lizard?"

Yoyo giggled again. "I hide my toys there so I can find something to play with if I wake up at night," she explained.

Maria had to laugh. "You don't wake up at night to play, silly. You sleep all night." She reached back under the covers and pulled out one more thing. A book. Her missing library book!

"Yoyo, you had my book!"

"I liked the pictures," Yoyo said in a sleepy voice. Maria started to say more, but instead she kissed Yoyo goodnight and turned out the light. Then she sat there for a minute, thinking and holding her book.

"Thank You, God," she said in a whisper. Then she ran down the hall to show her mother.

QUESTIONS

1. Do you lose library books like Maria did?

2. What else have you lost?

3. Did you know that God loves to help us when we ask?

4. Can you think of a time when God helped you find something?

5. Do you have faith like Elisha? Ask God to give you more faith.

CHAPTER

NAAMAN IS HEALED
Patti the Pain

During the time of Elisha, the country of Israel and the country of Syria were enemies. Many times, Syria's army attacked Israel and captured people. They took these people back to Syria to be slaves.

One little girl from Israel was a slave in the home of Naaman, the commander of the Syrian army. Naaman was a very powerful man, but he was sick. He had a terrible skin disease called leprosy. When the little girl heard about Naaman's disease, she spoke to Naaman's wife. "I wish my master Naaman could see the prophet in Samaria. God's prophet could heal him."

Naaman's wife told him what the girl had said. He went straight to his king. "There is a prophet in Israel who can heal people with leprosy. Let me go to see him."

The king of Syria agreed. He sent gifts of gold and silver with Naaman. Naaman traveled to Israel and went to see the king. "I have come to be healed of leprosy," he told the king.

The king got upset. "I'm not God," he said. "I can't heal people. Are you trying to start another war?"

But before anything could happen, the king got a message from Elisha. "Why are you getting so upset?" the message said. "Send Naaman to me."

So Naaman and all his men and all his gifts went to Elisha's house. When he got there, Elisha did not come out to meet him. Instead, a messenger gave Naaman this message. "Go and dip yourself in the Jordan River seven times, and you will be healed."

The message made Naaman mad. "We have better rivers in Syria. Why would I want to wash in this one? And Elisha was rude—he didn't even come out and talk to me." Naaman was so mad that he decided just to go straight home.

But along the way, his servants talked to him. "Master Naaman, if the prophet had given you something hard to do, you would have done it. Is this too easy? We're here anyway. Why not do what Elisha said to do? What can it hurt?"

Finally, Naaman agreed to do it. He went down to the Jordan River even though it was small. He waded out into the water even though it was dirty. He dipped down under the water six times, then once more. When he stood up this time, his skin was pink and healthy! He was healed!

Naaman rushed back to Elisha to thank him and give him gifts. "Now I know that there is a real God in heaven. I will worship only Him from now on," he said.

Elisha was happy. He wanted Naaman to learn about God and believe in Him. "I don't want any of your gifts or money," he told Naaman. "I work for God. Go home and be happy."

Gehazi, Elisha's servant, heard this. "*I* want some of that money," he said to himself. So he followed Naaman down the road and stopped him. "Some students from the schools of the prophets have just arrived at Elisha's house, and they need money," he lied.

Naaman was so happy about being healed that he gave Gehazi twice as much money as he asked for. Gehazi hurried home and hid the money so Elisha wouldn't know.

But Elisha knew. "Where have you been?" he asked Gehazi.

Gehazi lied again. "I didn't go anywhere," he answered.

Elisha shook his head sadly. "God showed me where you went. We don't take rewards for God's work. Now instead of rewards from Naaman, you will receive Naaman's disease."

And Gehazi had leprosy from that day on.

The little slave girl was unselfish. She wanted to help Naaman even though he was a Syrian—the people who had captured her and taken her far from her family. Gehazi wanted money for himself. His selfishness and lies brought him Naaman's disease.

Patti the Pain

"Then Patti wandered farther down the mall, all by herself, until she could no longer see her parents. Suddenly, two men jumped out and grabbed her. Before she could scream, they covered her mouth and dragged her to a black van waiting in the parking lot. Patti was kidnapped!"

When Mrs. Shue said that, Jenny's eyes flew open wide, her hand covered her mouth, and she fell back into her seat. The rest of the Shoebox Kids laughed out loud. Jenny looked at Mrs. Shue.

"Did I do that right?" she asked.

Mrs. Shue was laughing too. "You did it just right, Jenny. You acted just like you were being kidnapped."

When Mrs. Shue had first asked Jenny to be in a skit about the Hebrew maid, Jenny thought it would be boring. Everyone knew the story. The Hebrew maid was a servant to Naaman's wife. When Naaman got leprosy, the maid told him to go to the prophet Elisha and be healed. Naaman did, and he was healed.

But Mrs. Shue was making them think about the story as if it were happening today to someone like them, someone named Patti. There was a girl in Jenny's class at school whose name was Patti. Everyone called her "Patti the Pain."

"Patti was taken to another country far from her family and friends and forced to work all day with no pay. Her boss was a rich lady who just lay around, waiting to be served. All day long, Patti was vacuuming, sweeping, and washing dishes."

Maria played the part of the rich lady. She leaned back and raised her hand, waiting for someone to paint her fingernails.

"Now, Patti had a choice." When Mrs. Shue said this, she nodded to Sammy and Chris. They stood on each side of Jenny and read their parts.

"If this terrible thing could happen to me, then God must not care about me. Or else God is not real. I'll never believe in God again," Sammy read.

Chris read next. "I don't know why all this happened to me, but I need God now more than ever. I'm glad I learned to follow Him. Maybe He can make something good happen from this."

Jenny just listened as Mrs. Shue went on. "Patti chose to keep following God. She learned to trust God more and to pray and talk to Him more. Even though she worked in the house of the general who had sent the kidnappers out to her city, she didn't give up on God. She kept doing her work faithfully."

Mrs. Shue nodded at Sammy and Chris again. "Then Patti heard that the general had a disease and was going to die. She had another choice to make."

Sammy read first again. "Good! I'm glad he's going to die. He deserves to suffer after what he did to me. I just know that God is punishing him."

Then Chris read. "I wish the general knew more about God. God could heal him. I don't know why God put me here, but I know that He would want me to tell the general about Him."

Mrs. Shue read again. "We know that the general went to learn more about God and was healed. We don't know what happened to Patti. What would you have done in her place?" With that question, Mrs. Shue stood up and ended the skit. "Would you look like the Hebrew maid in Jesus' Mirror? Could you be as faithful and unselfish as she was?"

Later that week at school, Jenny remembered Mrs. Shue's story because the real Patti, Patti the Pain, was bothering her. It was art time, and the class was painting with watercolors. Jenny was carefully painting a picture of a sailboat on a deep blue sea, sailing into a red sunset.

"Let me see! What are you painting? What is that supposed to be?" Patti's questions came faster than Jenny could answer them, even if she wanted to. And she wasn't sure that she did. Especially with Patti hanging over her shoulder, bumping her arm.

"Patti, aren't you supposed to be working on your own painting?" Jenny wanted to be nice, but Patti was bothering her. "I'll tell you what mine is when I'm finished." She wasn't sure that her painting would really look like a sailboat on the sea at sunset when she was done.

Mr. Padgett spoke up. "Patti, please go back to your own work. It's only a few minutes until lunch. And today we are having chocolate mint ice-cream pie for dessert!"

"Ooooh!" Everyone in the room started whispering about their favorite dessert. Then they started painting faster. Even Patti went back to finish her painting. But after only a few minutes, Jenny heard that voice again.

"It's a jet airplane, isn't it? You're painting an airplane in the sky."

"Patti, let me finish, please. You're crowding my space," Jenny said. She saw that Mr. Padgett was headed toward them, but Patti just kept on talking.

"What's that red thing? Is it a cloud? You should have painted it white." Patti reached for the white paint and bumped the jar of red paint. Jenny reached for it, but it was too late.

Splat! Red paint was on the floor, on Jenny's shoes, on Patti's shoes, and on Mr. Padgett's shoes. He had walked up just in time to get splattered. "Patti, I asked you to stay at your place and do your own work. Now look at this mess. Get the rags and start wiping it up." Mr. Padgett looked very annoyed.

"But it's lunch time now. Can I clean it up after lunch?" Patti asked.

"No. It would be a dry mess by then. Clean it now. You'll just have to be last in line for lunch. Jenny, clean off your shoes at the sink before you leave. The rest of you can line up to go."

By the time Jenny got to the cafeteria, she was at the end of the line. Patti was nowhere in sight. Jenny peeked around at the dessert bar. The chocolate mint ice-cream pie was going fast. Since everyone wanted some, it might run out before she got there.

Her friend, Heather, was just picking up her pie. "Too bad Patti the Pain got paint on your shoes. I hope there's still some left when you get there," she called back to Jenny. "Come sit at my table when you get your food."

As she got closer, Jenny began to count the number of bowls left on the dessert bar. Then she counted the number of people in front of her. She counted twice and broke into a big smile. She would get the last piece!

Just as she was getting her food, Patti raced up behind her. "I hope I'm not too late for dessert. I love that ice-cream pie." Jenny didn't say anything. She stopped at the dessert bar and looked at the last bowl of chocolate and green mint swirl. It was hers. She picked it up just as Patti rushed to the bar.

"Is it all gone?"

Jenny hesitated only a second. "No, this is the last piece. You can have it. I don't think I want any today." Then she marched away to Heather's table before Patti could say a word.

"Where's your pie?" was Heather's first question. "Did you let that pain Patti have the last one? After what she did in art class? Why?"

Jenny shrugged her shoulders. "Because I'm a Christian. And being a Christian means being nice to people, even when they are a pain." Heather stared at her.

Jenny just smiled back at her. Then she drank her milk and thought to herself, *I don't know if I look like the Hebrew maid, but I think I know how she felt.*

QUESTIONS

1. How would you feel if you were kidnapped and taken from your parents and friends?

2. Why would it be hard to keep believing in God and trusting Him?

3. Is there someone in your school like Patti the Pain?

4. How can being unselfish be a witness?

12
CHAPTER

ELISHA SHOWS GOD'S POWER
Angels in a Station Wagon

The schools of the prophets were growing fast. When Elisha visited the one at Jericho, he stayed to help them build a bigger room for classes. The students borrowed all the axes they could find. They carried the axes with their heavy iron heads down to the trees near the Jordan River.

Elisha went with the tree cutters. He watched as the students swung their axes and trees fell. Then as one student was swinging, the iron head flew off his ax and right out into the river!

"Oh, no," he cried. "I borrowed that ax, and it is very valuable. What will I do?"

Elisha stepped up. "Where did it fall?" he asked.

"Right there," the student said, pointing to a spot in the river. Maybe Elisha was going to wade out and try to find it. But instead, Elisha did something very strange. He cut a stick off a tree limb and threw it out into the water where the ax head had disappeared.

And the heavy iron ax head floated right up to the top of the water!

The student just stood there with his mouth hanging open. Finally, Elisha said, "Pick it up." The student snatched it out of the water and went back to work.

Another time, the king of Syria was fighting Israel again. He planned a surprise attack that would defeat Joram, the king of Israel, and his army. But when he got there, Israel's army wasn't there. Every time he tried to trap the Israelites, they found out about it and escaped.

Finally, the king of Syria called his captains together. "One of you is a spy!" he shouted as he pounded on the table. "Every time I plan an attack, someone tells the king of Israel. Who is the spy?"

"There is no spy," one of the men explained. "Elisha, the prophet in Israel, tells King Joram everything you plan." It was true. Elisha warned King Joram many times about where the Syrian army was going.

"We need to catch Elisha and kill him," the king of Syria decided. He found out that Elisha was staying in the city of Dothan, so he sent a large army to surround the city.

When Elisha's servant saw all those soldiers around the city, he was afraid. "What can we do, master?" he cried.

"Don't be afraid," Elisha said. "The army that fights for us is much bigger than the one that has us surrounded." Then he prayed, "Lord, let my servant see Your army."

Suddenly, the servant could see why Elisha was not afraid. An army of angels, with chariots and horses made of fire, stood between them and the Syrians!

Then the Syrian army began to march toward the city. Elisha prayed, "Make these soldiers blind." And God made all the army of Syria blind. Elisha went out on the road in front of the city and said, "This is not the road you want. This is not the city you are looking for. Come, I will lead you to the man you are looking for."

Then Elisha led them to Samaria, where King Joram and his whole army waited. When they were inside the city, Elisha prayed, "Lord, open their eyes." When they looked around, the Syrians saw that they were inside Israel's capital city!

King Joram asked Elisha, "Should I kill them all?"

"No," Elisha answered, "don't kill them. Have a banquet, feed them, then send them home." So that's what happened. After a big party, the Syrians went home happy. And those soldiers never came back to fight with Israel again.

With God's power, Elisha was able to take care of little problems and big problems. God loves to use His power to help His people.

Angels in a Station Wagon

"It's a moose!"

"No, it's two mooses."

Chris and Maria crowded to see out the window on one side. The two animals raced away into the dark woods.

The Vargas family was on a camping trip. Chris, Maria, Yoyo, and their parents had spent the Sabbath hiking and picnicking in the mountains. Now on their way back to their campsite, they had their eyes open for wildlife.

"Let's stop here at this overlook and watch the sunset turn to stars," Mrs. Vargas suggested. They pulled over and parked. Chris and Maria got out and watched. Yoyo closed her eyes and stayed in her seat. When they were ready to go, Mr. Vargas turned the car key, but nothing happened.

"What's wrong?" Chris asked.

"It's not starting. I'd better look under the hood." Mr. Vargas got out with his flashlight. Soon the hood slammed, and he climbed back in. "Well, the good news is, it will be easy to fix. The bad news is, the wire I need to fix it is in my toolbox. And we left that at the campsite."

"So here we sit." Mrs. Vargas looked worried. Chris and Maria looked worried too.

"If we could just make it over this last steep rise, we could coast down to the campsite," Dad said. "The battery isn't dead, so we would still have lights."

Chris looked around at the darkening sky. Maria was doing the same thing. They looked at each other and nodded. Chris opened the car door. "Let's try to push it," he said.

"OK, let's try. We'll push while you drive," Mr. Vargas said to his wife as they got out.

"Do you think that's a good idea?" she asked, sliding into the driver's seat.

"It's the only idea I have left," he answered. They got behind the car with their dad and counted. "One, two, three, push!" Mr. Vargas pushed until the sweat was rolling down his face. Maria pushed until she thought her arms were going to fall off. Chris pushed so hard he thought his eyeballs were going to pop out. But the car barely moved a few inches.

"Well, that won't work," Mr. Vargas admitted when they quit.

"I still have one idea," Mrs. Vargas said as they got back in the van. "Let's pray." And she did. "Father in heaven, please help us get back safely. Help us get our car over the mountain. Thank You, in Jesus' name. Amen."

For a few minutes after Mrs. Vargas had prayed for help, Chris and Maria listened while their parents talked about walking to find a house or store. Chris whispered to Maria, "I don't remember any houses or stores along this road. We'd have to walk a long way."

"I see a car," Yoyo said from her seat.

"Yoyo, I thought you were asleep," Maria said.

"I see a car," Yoyo repeated, pointing backward. Chris looked and saw two headlights shining in the dark.

"It *is* a car. Coming from behind us," he almost shouted. Everyone turned and watched as the lights got closer. Soon they could see an old, beat-up station wagon. It stopped behind them, and two men stepped out. Mr. Vargas walked back to meet them.

As the men stepped into the beam of their headlights, Chris could see that they looked pretty beat-up too. They had old, dirty clothes and scruffy, dirty faces. He noticed his mother lean over and lock the car door.

"You folks got some kind of trouble?" The scruffy face spoke in a kind voice.

"Yes. Our car died, and it won't start. If we could just get over this next rise, we could coast back to our campsite. We're staying over in Bear Tooth Campground." Mr. Vargas spoke in a friendly way as he explained. "Do you have a chain or rope that could pull us?"

The man looked over at his partner, who shook his head. "No, I guess we don't. But we could push you if our bumpers match up."

Mr. Vargas wasn't too sure about that. "I don't think so. The bumpers on this car are probably lower than those on your station wagon."

"Let's try it and see," the man said and got into his station wagon. He pulled right up close behind the car, until the bumpers were nearly touching.

"How about that! They are about the same height," Mr. Vargas said. "Are you sure you want do this? If we move apart just a little and crash back together, it might damage your car."

"It'll be fine. Let's give it a try," the man said. Mr. Vargas got back in.

"Are they going to help us?" Chris asked.

"They're going to push us. Be sure your seat belts are fastened. It could be bumpy." He released the brakes, and put the shifter in neutral.

"Are you sure this is a good idea?" Mrs. Vargas asked.

"Even if it damages the bumper some, it won't cost any more than having a tow truck or someone come and get us. And this way we might get back tonight." As he was speaking, the station wagon bumped the back, and then they were moving slowly up the hill.

The car picked up speed as it was pushed faster. Then a little dip in the road made it move ahead of the station wagon. Everyone held their breath, hoping that the car would keep rolling. But it slowed down and the station wagon moved up from behind again.

"Hold on for a bump," Mr. Vargas said. Maria grabbed Yoyo. The station wagon hit their bumper with a "thud," and they were rolling faster again. This time they stayed close to the car until they zipped over the top of the mountain.

"Here we go," Mr. Vargas exclaimed. They pulled ahead of the station wagon and rolled swiftly down the slope.

"We're going to make it!" Mom said. "It's all downhill from here." Chris stared back at the station wagon that was following at a distance.

"I wish we could stop and thank them," Maria said.

"It wouldn't be smart to stop now," her dad answered. "Besides, I don't remember any place to pull over until we get back to the campground. If they stop, we'll get to say thanks."

"They're gone," Chris said.

"What?" Maria turned around and looked.

"They're not there now. Their lights just went out." Chris just kept looking back to where they had been.

"But they have to be," Maria said. "There was no place to turn, was there? And no houses where they could have stopped." She didn't understand.

Chris thought he did. "They must have been angels God sent to help us."

ELISHA SHOWS GOD'S POWER

For a minute, no one said a word. Maria's mouth was hanging open like a flytrap. Then their mom said quietly, "Well, we did ask God to help us."

When they got back to the campsite, Chris and Maria and their dad went back to look at the car's bumper. "There's not a scratch or a dent," Mr. Vargas said.

"Do you really think they were angels, Dad?" Maria asked.

"They could have been. We won't know for sure until we get to heaven," he answered. "But we do know that we asked for help, and God helped us. He sent either angels or just nice people to help us get back to our campsite."

"We'll sure have something to tell our Shoebox friends when we get home," Chris said. "God really does use His power to help us when we ask."

QUESTIONS

1. Do you like camping? Do you have a favorite camping spot?

2. Do you remember to pray when you need help?

3. Did you know that sometimes God sends angels to help us? Sometimes He sends people to help us too.

13

THE RUNAWAY ARMY
Willie Forgets Coco!

There was a new king in Syria, and he attacked Israel again. This time, Samaria was surrounded, and no one could get in or out. There was almost no food left in the city, and it cost a lot of money for just a mouthful. People were beginning to die of hunger.

King Joram was very angry. He blamed the hunger on Elisha and on God. "These problems are Elisha's fault," he said. "I will have him killed today."

Elisha was in his house talking to some of the other leaders of the city. He said, "The king has sent someone to kill me, and he is just outside. Hold the door shut and keep him out. Don't worry, the king is coming right behind him."

So the men held the door shut until King Joram showed up. "This is God's fault," the king said. "Why should I trust Him any longer."

Elisha shook his head. "By tomorrow, you will be able to buy seven quarts of flour or thirteen quarts of barley for just a little silver."

THE RUNAWAY ARMY

The king and his head officer both laughed. They knew that there was no flour or barley in the whole city. The officer said, "Even if God Himself opened the windows of heaven and poured out flour, it wouldn't be that cheap."

Elisha was sad. "You will see this happen," he told the officer. "But you won't get to eat any of the food."

That same day, four men with leprosy—a terrible skin disease—were sitting outside the city gates. They hadn't eaten any food for days. "Let's not just sit here until we die," one of them said. "Let's go over to the enemy's camp. If they kill us—oh, well, we were going to die anyway. But maybe they will give us some food."

So the men went to where the army of Syria had set up all their tents. But no one was there! The whole camp was still standing—all the tents, all the horses, all the supplies, and all the food were still there!

During the night, God had made the soldiers from Syria hear a very loud noise. It sounded like horses and chariots and soldiers. "The king of Israel has hired the army of Egypt to attack us," they cried. And they ran away without taking anything with them.

The four men couldn't believe it. First they ate and drank as much as they could hold. Then they took some gold and silver and hid it. Finally, they said, "We have to tell the king about this. We have to tell everyone what has happened!"

So they ran back to Samaria and shouted to the guards. "The enemy army is gone! They ran away and left everything in their camp!"

The guards passed the message on to the king. "It must be a trick," the king said. "They're waiting for us to come out, and then they'll attack."

One of the king's officers said, "Let's send some men out on horses to find out. We're all going to die soon anyway." So the king sent out some soldiers to find the enemy army. But they couldn't find anyone.

The king sent his head officer out to guard the city gate. Soon the people in the city began to hear the story of the empty camp. When they heard about the food, they rushed out of the city gate. So many people rushed out so quickly that the officer at the gate was crushed.

It happened just as Elisha had promised it would. There was plenty of food in Samaria again, and it was cheap to buy. But the king's head officer didn't live to eat any of it. God rescued His people again, just as Elisha promised He would.

Willie Forgets Coco!

"**Y**ou don't mind staying at your grandparents' house this weekend, do you, Willie?"

"No, Mom. I like staying at Grandma's. She said we were going to do some fun things, like go to the museum's discovery center for kids and go to ShowTime Pizza. I like to spend weekends with Grandma and Grandpa," Willie answered.

His mother pulled another shirt from his drawer and packed it into the suitcase. "They'll take you to school and to Sabbath School on Sabbath, so you won't miss anything. Now, shall I take Coco to a kennel? That's what I told Grandma we would do."

Willie dropped his toothbrush and comb into the suitcase. "No. I promise to take care of him. He'll be happier here in his own yard. I'll come by every day and bring him food and water."

"You'll have to ask Grandma to pick up some dog food at the grocery store. We're out, and I forgot to get some last night. I'll finish packing. You promised to have your playroom cleaned up before you left."

Willie rolled out and down the hall to his playroom. Looking in, he had to admit that it was a mess. The table was covered with half-colored papers and markers. His desk was covered with upside-down cars and trucks, still where he had left them after their big race yesterday. It had ended with a big crash. The cars and trucks were still crashed.

So I promised to clean this up, Willie thought. *Well, then, I'd better get busy. And what else did I promise to do? Oh, yes, give Coco food and water this weekend.* "Mom," he called, "are you sure Coco can't go with me?"

He heard his mother's voice from the other room. "Willie, you know that Grandma's yard doesn't have a fence. Coco would have to be on a leash all day. He'd be happier here in his own yard or in a kennel."

Willie knew she was right, but leaving Coco was the only thing he didn't like about going to his grandparents'. He got busy putting his markers and cars back into their places. He was surprised when his mother called him.

"Willie, they're here. Grab your suitcase and come on."

Willie Forgets Coco!

He rolled out to the door and smiled at his grandmother. "Hi, Grandma," he said. "Bye, Mom. Tell Dad goodbye for me. Have fun on your trip."

On the way to their house, Willie quizzed his grandparents about their plans. "Are we going to the museum? When?"

"Yes, we are going to the museum. That will be Thursday afternoon. Then, you still have school on Friday and Sabbath School the next day."

"What about ShowTime Pizza?" It was Willie's favorite place to eat in the world. It had shows and programs and games. And great pizza!

"We'll go there Friday after school. I promise!" Grandpa said with a big smile. "Now, slow down a little. I'm getting tired just thinking about all the things you want to do."

Willie's time with his grandparents went fast. He stayed busy all the time. By the time school was out on Friday afternoon, he was ready for some pizza. When his grandparents picked him up, he started asking.

"Are we going to ShowTime Pizza now?"

"Not yet," his grandma answered with a laugh. "But soon. We have one stop to make, and then we'll go."

Willie sat back and quietly watched the cars go by— for about one minute. Then he had more questions. "Where are we stopping?"

"We're stopping at the grocery store. We need more food if Grandma's going to keep you fed all weekend," Grandpa said as they stopped at a red light. "But then we'll go to the pizza place just like I promised."

Willie sat back in his chair again. He wasn't really thinking about it, but the words were floating in his head: grocery store, food, promise. *Did I forget something,* he wondered to himself. Then he remembered.

"Coco!"

Grandma and Grandpa both turned and looked at him. For a second, he just stared back at them with his eyes open wide. Finally, it came out. "I promised to take care of Coco."

"I thought Coco was in a kennel," Grandma said.

"No. I told Mom that he would be happier in his own yard. I promised to give him his food and water." Willie was really upset now. "I promised."

Grandma reached back and patted him. Grandpa said, "Didn't your mother give him some food and water before she left?"

Willie shook his head sadly. "I'm sure she filled his water bowl, but I was supposed to ask you to buy some food for him that first night. Now he hasn't had any food for two whole days."

The light turned green, and they drove on. Willie reached up and grabbed his grandpa's arm. "Can we go and feed him now? I don't care about ShowTime Pizza."

Grandpa nodded his head. "We'll have to go on to the grocery store and buy him some food. But we'll shop quickly and go straight back to your house."

Willie thought it would take them forever to get all their food, but he didn't say anything. He knew they were hurrying as fast as they could. As soon as his wheels were on the ground, he headed for the gate to the backyard.

Willie Forgets Coco!

"Coco! Coco, are you there? Here, Coco," he called as he opened the gate. Just as the gate swung open, something hit him right in the chest. It was Coco! Willie's face was hit by a wet tongue. "Coco, you're OK!"

Grandpa brought in the food, and they watched while Coco ate and drank like crazy. Grandpa put his arm around Willie. "It's easy to forget. I'm glad you remembered your promise to take care of your friend Coco."

"I shouldn't have forgotten. I guess I'm not too good at keeping promises," Willie said.

"The only one who always keeps His promises is God. He promises to always love us, to protect us, and to take us to live with Him forever if we choose," Grandma reminded Willie.

Willie thought about that. "But what about when people get hurt or killed? Isn't God breaking His promise to protect them?"

"It's like my promise to take you to ShowTime Pizza. If I had known about Coco, and you didn't, you might have been unhappy that I brought you here instead of going to the pizza place."

Willie agreed. "But as soon as I knew about Coco, I would be glad that you did it."

"It's like that with God," Grandpa said. "If we knew everything He does, we would know why even the bad things happen. But we don't know, so we have to trust Him and believe His promises. He always does what He says He will do."

That Sabbath, Willie told his Shoebox friends about Coco and his promise. "But I'm glad I learned that God always keeps His promises."

Mrs. Shue smiled at her Shoebox Kids. "I know one promise that God kept this quarter. He promised that if we become friends with Jesus, we will become like Him. And all of you look more like Jesus than you did before."

The Shoebox Kids just looked at one another and smiled.

QUESTIONS

1. Do you have a pet like Coco? I hope you promise to always take care of it!

2. Do you always keep your promises?

3. Aren't you glad God always keeps His promises?

4. Do you look more like Jesus than you did before? Ask your teacher. Ask a parent. Ask anyone who knows you!

Real-life lessons from the Bible for today's kids.

Shoebox Kids Bible Stories

Jerry D. Thomas. As Sammy, Jenny, Willie, DeeDee, Chris, and Maria meet at church, they find that their Bible stories have a strange way of fitting into the things that happen to them each week! Their adventures will help your child learn how the Bible makes a difference at home, at school, or on the playground.

1. **Creation to Abraham.** Creation, the Sabbath, Cain and Abel, the Flood, Abraham and Isaac. Every chapter is a double story—one from the Bible, then a Shoebox story that applies the Bible lesson. Paper, 128 pages. 0-8163-1823-9.

2. **From Isaac to the Red Sea.** The Bible stories in this book start with Eliezar's search for a wife for Isaac, include Joseph's dreams, and end with the parting of the Red Sea and bread from heaven. Paper, 128 pages. 0-8163-1877-8.

3. **From the Ten Commandments to Jericho**. Water from the rock, the Ten Commandments, the golden calf, the brass serpent, Balaam's donkey, and crossing the Jordan. Paper, 128 pages. 0-8163-1911-1.

4. **From Joshua to David, Goliath, and Jonathan.** Joshua gets tricked by the Gibeonites, the day the sun stood still, Samson defeats the Philistines, and David battles Goliath. Paper, 128 pages. 0-8163-1949-9.